MAEVE

Josh Dygert

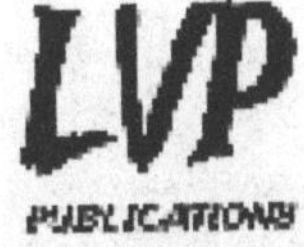

Lycan Valley Press Publications
1002 N Meridian STE 100-153
Puyallup, Washington 98371
United States of America

First Edition

ISBN-13: 978-1-64562-043-3

MAEVE

CHAPTER 1

MOUNTAIN SKIES CAN be beautiful. They can look as big as the world. In the mountains, you can tell yourself that nothing else exists at all. That you are the only person in the entire world. It's the loneliest feeling that I've ever known. And sometimes, it's a loneliness that drives me mad. And sometimes, it's a loneliness that gives me peace. It is always, somehow, both. Even in the madness, there's that little bit of peace. And in that peace, there's always a little bit of the madness.

I grew up in the mountains. Where it's cold. But where it's beautiful. There, the evergreen trees stand quiet sentry to the passing of the years. Ever present, unchanging guardsmen of my childhood. They were there at the beginning, and they were there at the end. They saw my first steps, and they saw the moment that I lost my childhood and left those mountains forever.

It was always just me and Dad.

Mom disappeared…or left…or died, I never knew which, when I was very young. I only have one memory of my mother. I don't even know for sure that it's not just a dream or a fantasy that I've made up based on what people have told me over the years. But it feels real.

It's just me and her. And we're laying out by the ridge down in the woods behind my house. We're lying inside of snow angels, a mother angel and a daughter angel.

And we're just looking up at the stars. Out there, if the sky was clear, you could see the stars like they were right there, hanging just out of reach like an infant's mobile hovering over the crib of the Earth. They were more than stars. They were alive. And the whole sky and the whole wood and the whole mountain glittered in the light of their songshine.

And as we lay there, one star fell from the sky.

I turned to my mother and watched her face as she tracked the falling of the star. The ends of her hair escaped the confines of her hat. Her cheeks were pink. Her eyes shone with the light of that falling star.

"You see that star?" she asked, pointing it out to me.

"I do," I said.

"They say that shooting stars are magic," she

said. "Some people think that they have extra wishing powers. Other people think that they're alive."

I smiled up at my mother and at the star, the light of which shone on her face.

"What do you think it is, Momma?" I asked.

"I think you better make a wish," she said.

And I did. I wish I could tell you that I wished for something beautiful and meaningful. But I didn't. I wished to have superpowers. Or a magic sword. Or a flying horse.

Maybe if I'd wished for something possible, my wish might have come true.

Maybe if I'd wished for my mother to stay, she might have stayed.

But I must have been barely old enough to talk, let alone comprehend that I needed to wish for things like mothers who stayed and didn't leave their husbands and little girls.

Now, I know exactly what I'd wish for.

Dad didn't like to talk about Mom. He would. But he had a rule. I could ask whatever I wanted about her but never on February the 24th. Never on the anniversary of the day she vanished…or left… or died. It was an easy rule to follow. And before long, I was far too overwhelmed at the mere thought of my mother and of our loss to ask any longer. Sometimes, I was angry. I didn't know for sure that she had left of her own accord, but it can be hard to remain fair in the presence of her absence. But I never did let go of that one shining, shooting star of a memory of her. It was the one thing the anger could never touch.

My dad was a man of many loves. He loved the mountains, and he loved his art. He loved making things and building things and designing things. He loved smooth wood and bonfires and good wine. He loved painting and carving and carpentry. He loved drawing and books and old movies. He loved vinyl records and Twix bars and Audrey Hepburn. He loved my friends, Rosa and Iris. He loved his friends, and he loved our house.

But my dad loved three things most of all. He loved my mother, me, and the mountains.

I grew up walking the trails. I grew up knowing the points of a compass and how to find my way home by the stars. I knew the woods around our house like the back of my hand. And I never knew a time when I didn't.

But there was one place in the woods I never went. Where my father never took me.

CHAPTER 2

I GREW UP hearing the legends since before I can remember.

On those long, cold nights after my mother vanished, I gathered my two best friends beside me. My father would light a fire in the hearth, and we would gather around it as he lit another kind of fire with his words. All those nights blend together into one night. One long night where the flames from the chimney and the flames inside the hearts of my friends and the warmth of my father's story, would serve to keep at bay the bitter frost of the shadows at the door.

All my life, I had two best friends.

The three of us have been best friends since before my memory begins. We called ourselves the three musketeers because my father was always reading us adventure tales, and his favorite tale was *The Three Musketeers*. It was his favorite tale because it was my mother's favorite tale when she was a child. He read it to us from my mother's copy. It had been hers when she was a little girl, and so we three dreamed of growing up and fighting for truth, honor, and love. Just like my mother had.

On my left hand side on those nights, there would always be Iris.

Iris O'Hannon lived next door. She had long, brittle, white blonde hair and blue, crystal eyes. She was a very serious little girl, even in those early days. When I thought of her in those early days, I thought of butterfly nets and firefly jars. I thought of books bigger than a little girl's head and facts after facts after facts.

Her parents didn't know what to do with a girl like her. Her parents were always so in love. Her father was an elementary school teacher, and her mother was an interior designer. They liked art and alcohol and laughter. And they never quite understood why their daughter was so entranced with numbers. They never quite got the seriousness in her eyes. Why there was always something frozen in her.

But when she was by my side. When the fire lit our big living room, when it illuminated her eyes, they seemed to glow with the firelight. And she seemed to thaw. The light would send the shadows of all my father's carved figurines upon the wall and make them dance like the characters in the stories he would tell us or read to us.

And Iris was always the last to laugh at the funny parts, but when she did, the sound of her voice was like the sound of her piano playing. Joyful and musical and warm and good.

And by my right side, there was Rosa A'Hearn. Rosa's hair was as dark as Iris's was light. And her eyes always shimmered with a strange kind of warmth. She had constellations of freckles, and her hair grew in ebbing waves and inconsistent curls.

Rosa could be timid. Rosa could be quiet. But of all of us, she was the first to laugh. And the first to hug. And the first to cry.

Rosa, unlike me, had two parents. And yet, unlike me and Iris, it was like she had none. Rosa never spoke about her parents. She never spoke about her house. She never invited us over. And when she mentioned her mother and father, a bitter cold would sweep through her voice and into any room that we occupied.

But there by my side, in those nights with my father and the stories, Rosa was a shining star of warmth and light. She was always there for me.

All those nights were like one night, and that one night was the foundation of my life. It glowed and flickered with the light of flame and father and friendship.

Our bellies were usually full of pizza or chicken fingers and maybe some ice cream. And my father, my father who was a father to both of my friends, would tell us a story. Usually, he'd read to us from the Great Books, the ones about small, hurt people going on great adventures to become big, strong heroes.

But sometimes, he'd tell us our own story.

The story of our town, Dackett, and its ghost father, Morton.

Everyone knew the story, and every single family seemed to have a slightly different version. The bones were always the same, though.

And this is the story as my father told it to the three musketeers on those long ago, once upon a time sort of nights when the three of us were girls together and my father was all of our fathers.

"Once, a long time ago, up in the woods and the mountains that surrounded our valley town, there was another town," my father would say. My father had an excellent voice for stories. It was a voice full of deep valleys and high mountains, a voice that could boom and a voice that could whimper. It was just the right kind of voice for a fire. "A mining settlement back in the 1800s. For a while, the settlement boomed. Records indicate a huge influx of workers as the copper mines flourished. People came to the little town of Morton from all over during the Copper Rush. All reports indicate that the people of the mining town were happy. The man who ran the mine was famous for his beneficence and generosity. Hours and conditions were moderate and fair, especially for that day and age."

Depending on how old we were, we might press him on this. If we'd learned about the Industrial Revolution and the mines in school, we might question him, but he'd always insist.

"No, no, Morton wasn't like that. Morton knew better. Always. Even before the world learned, it knew. It was a place for families. The kind of place in which all the conditions were ripe for growth and continued growth. There were even rumors of the railroad coming to town."

And we three would sit and dream of a town about to boom, a town about to dream itself into reality.

"Until, one day, out of nowhere, the town simply ceased to be.

"No one knows how it happened. No one knows exactly when. But on March 27, 1881, a shipment of goods arrived from out of town at the local general store. The delivery man was the son of the family who ran the store. When he'd left the town on March 25th, everything had been normal. As far as anyone knows, March 25th was the last time that anyone saw the town alive and well."

Beside me, Rosa would shudder. And then I would shudder. And Iris would shudder. Like falling, shuddering dominoes.

"Delivery man Bob Dackett did not waste time. From the moment he'd entered the town, he'd known something was wrong. The town of Morton was always bustling with life. You couldn't make your way from one end of Main Street to the Dackett General without encountering at least seven people you knew and stopping to talk to at least four, no matter what you had in the back of the cart or how tired the horses were."

"Sounds like Dackett now," Rosa muttered.

And my father would smile. "Yes," he'd say. "Exactly like Dackett. But that morning, Bob Dackett didn't encounter a single soul. What's more, no matter where you were in the town, you could always see smoke rising from the mines, and you could always hear the grating and growling of machinery at this time of day. But that day, there was silence."

And my father would pause, and the three of us would become very conscious of the sound of our breath in that long, quiet pause where only the fire dared speak in its crackling log voice.

"A silence that struck Bob Dackett as the most terrifying sound he'd ever heard. At least, that's how I imagine he must have felt. As he passed the baker's, there was no smell of bread."

And we, we who would have gorged ourselves on pizza, we who could still smell the pizza on the air and on our breath, would shrink at that.

"As he passed the butcher's, there was the smell of meat gone rotten." And I would curl my toes and squinch my face, and if I looked to the left and to the right, I'd see that Iris and Rosa wore the same squinched faces. And if I'd glanced down at all of our toes, I dare say they'd all have been curled in identical disgust.

"And as he entered the town square, the old church tower bell stared down at him. It should have rung. It was time for it to ring, judging by the clock hands pointing to nine o'clock. But it was silent."

Again, he let that silence stretch. Again, only the fire log spoke in its crackling tongue. And maybe, just maybe, I could hear the ticking of a clock on the wall. Or the scratch of my own breath in my lungs.

"Bob pulled up outside the family general store, but he didn't unhitch the horses or bother with the supplies he'd brought all the way from Marquette.

"No. He went straight into the shop.

"He pulled open the wooden door. The bell jingled.

"The shop was just as he'd left it. Not a thing was changed.

"There was the counter where townsfolk would order their supplies, and behind the counter, the shelves of food and goods.

"'Ma?' he called."

And again, my father would wait at this point in the story, as if he, too, were Bob, waiting on some response from his own Ma.

"No answer. Ma was always in the shop at that

time of day.

"'Pa?' he called."

Again, my father paused. And again, we held our breath.

"No answer. But this time of day, Pa was usually out back, working in the yard.

"'Mary Lynne,' he called the name of his younger sister who was liable to be just about anywhere. She never did what she was told, and she never kept regular hours."

And here, he would pause, and I would have time enough to think that Mary Lynne was my favorite character in this story. I also did not believe in regular hours or doing as I was told.

"But Mary Lynne didn't answer either." And I would shudder to wonder what happened to my favorite character.

"Bob Dackett lifted the wooden plank that separated the customer's side of the store from the Dackett family side. He walked the several paces to the stairs at the back, his feet loud against the wooden floorboards.

"A quick look out the back windows told him no one, much less Pa, was out there. He pushed open the door next to the stairs. The kitchen was empty. But there were bowls on the table of half-eaten soup. In a daze, Bob Dackett went to the nearest bowl and swirled a finger through it.

"Cold."

And again, the domino of cold shudders would

run from Rosa to me to Iris.

"No one was there.

"He ran to the center of the town square and turned a circle all around him. There was the police station. Empty. There was the town hall. Empty. There was the post office. Empty. There was the church, towering above every other building in town with its spire that reached toward the ice gray sky.

"Empty.

"All empty.

"Everyone was gone.

"And so Bob Dackett ran to his little cart with its two horses without bothering to unload his supplies. Without stopping to feed his horses. He jumped inside, and he urged the horses on.

"And he didn't stop until he reached the next outposting.

"The rest is history. The authorities of 1881, local, state, and federal, all came to the little mining town of Morton in response to poor Bob Dackett. And they all found the town just as Dackett said.

"Empty."

And here, he would pause once again. And we would wait because the story wasn't done, not quite. And we knew it.

"Well, almost empty. There was one survivor. There was a man who had been deep in the mines when it happened.

"When authorities found him, he wouldn't stop raving. He told a tale of a meteor shower. Of emerging from the mines to find everyone in town cocooned in strange light. Of course, he was put in a madhouse, where he spent the rest of his days."

And the three of us musketeers would glance from left to right to left, and we would think…here it is. Here's the answer. He wasn't mad. He knew the truth. Meteors and cocoons of light and mystery and magic. All of it, the stuff of our childhoods.

"Theories grew up surrounding the town in the years since then. Some said they were snatched away by fairies. Others by the spirits of the mountains. Twentieth century versions had the whole town abducted by aliens, and, briefly, by time traveling Russian Communists or astral projecting German Nazis. But whatever theory, whatever version of the story was told, some facts, gathered from diaries and journals, inventories and receipts, were always the same."

And here we would lean in, as if upon being given the recitation of facts, we three musketeers would be the ones to finally understand, to finally put together the answer.

"On the morning of March 26th, there was a meteor shower. It was noted in at least eight different journals. And beyond that morning of March 26th, there was nothing. Beyond the meteor shower, not a single further diary entry, receipt, sale logged, nothing.

"Not until Bob Dackett arrived on March 27th with his cart full of groceries.

"And there stands the great mystery of the Dackett Woods."

Somewhere out there in the woods that stretched out beyond my house, there was a ghost town. Overgrown and abandoned.

And we would all feel it there. As if it were a living thing. We would feel it at our shoulders, right behind us, listening to its story, just as we listened.

"The roads that once led to Morton grew over long ago. The plans to build a railroad, if plans had ever evolved beyond rumor, were scrapped. Now, the only way to Morton is a deep trek through cold, snowy woods. Sometimes, researchers and photographers go out there. And maybe a high school kid or two. But only the stupid ones. Mostly, no one does. It's a sad sort of place. The kind of place that remembers its sorrow."

At least, that's what my Dad always said when he told the story. He swore he never went, but I think that he lied.

"And so it was that the town of Morton passed into memory, and the town of Dackett got its start. Because Bob Dackett's story did not end that day in March. It had only begun. Bob Dackett married the daughter of a wealthy businessman. He joined a small group of others who started a community right here. He started his own general store, and before long, he had ten children and had been elected mayor. The town loved him so much they decided to call themselves Dackett when they realized that they'd gone from a small spattering of houses to a true community. That's why we have a statue of Bob Dackett in our own town square.

"Maybe that's why the people of Dackett have never forgotten the town of Morton. Because Bob still stares down at us from ten feet of gleaming bronze whenever we go down Main Street. A constant reminder of the place from which we come. Of the tragedy from which we arose. The mystery that, to this day, haunts Bob and, therefore, the rest of us Dackettsonians."

And how that mystery haunted us. How we would exchange glances and bristle with the feeling of mystery and need. The need to know. The need to solve. The need for adventure.

And the three musketeers weren't alone.

For all my father's qualifications, the trek to Morton was, to the teenagers of Dackett, a rite of passage. Every teenager who was any teenager made the journey at least once before graduating from high school. And I knew my father too well to think that he had missed out on an adventure.

I supposed in his old age, he worried about his daughter getting lost in the woods or attacked by a bear or having a ceiling cave in on her in the old houses. I supposed that was why he lied.

But he should have known, even back in those early days, those days of mourning, of stories around the fire, that there was nothing he could say to prevent my going.

I wish there had been. But in those days, I was far too stubborn to listen to anything anyone told me. Far too close-minded to see just how foolish I was. Far too high on my own intelligence to realize that I'd yet to attain wisdom.

If I'd known, I would have done it all differently.

If I'd known, I would have let my curiosity rest.

But I didn't know. And if someone told me, I'd never have listened.

Because there at the bottom of everything was that story and those nights with my father and the three musketeers, shining, shimmering, gleaming like the north star in my memory.

And so it became my dearest wish, all the way back in those days following the disappearance of my mother, that I would one day go to Morton. And that I, and the three musketeers by my left and my right, would be the ones to solve the mystery.

It was all tied up with my mother.

Maybe if it wasn't, then maybe, I'd have been able to let go.

Then maybe, just maybe, everything wouldn't have ended in such disaster.

CHAPTER 3

THE THING IS that I did not believe that my mother had left.

My father never said she left.

He said only that she was gone. And he said it with such a horrible hurting in his hazel eyes that I could say no more, ask no more. And so I lived for year after year without the knowledge of what happened to her.

And in that absence, the anger grew.

But so, too, did the alternative.

And he told that tale of our ghost town so often, how could I not tie the two together? How could I not believe that whatever had taken Morton had taken my mother, too?

To solve one mystery was to solve them both.

And so I poured myself into the mystery.

I tried everything. I asked my teachers. I asked the people at church. I asked the neighbors. I asked my friends' parents. I asked the librarian.

Everyone always told a slightly different version of the same tale. And no one ever seemed to suspect that what I was really asking about was my mother. The librarian showed me newspaper articles from the time period, and they differed very little from what everyone had always told me.

And I knew…I knew, too, that my mother wasn't the only one.

Because I wasn't the only musketeer missing a parent.

To misplace a sock or a pen is common enough. Most people do. To misplace a parent, though, is a little more unusual. But not in Dackett. In Dackett, I wasn't the only one to misplace a parent.

I can never pinpoint the year without having to stop and think. I was old enough to know, old enough to remember viscerally that night and the days that followed. So that meant I was a lot older than I was when my mother vanished, but I was still young.

I think it happened when I was five.

It happened in January.

There was a meteor shower that night, too.

I remember thinking how beautiful it all was. That night was the first time I remember thinking how beauty could hide something terrible, although I guess that was a lesson I already should have known.

The musketeers assembled that night to watch the stars fall. We ate pizza, and we went to bed.

And we woke the next morning to the kind of news that you spend your whole life trying never to get. This time, it was Iris that the news came for.

The facts were these.

Iris's parents had enjoyed a date night. They'd gone to Sal's, the Italian restaurant in town. When they got home, they shared a bottle of wine, bundled up, and took a snowmobile ride out into the woods to find the best place to watch the stars fall.

Iris's mother swore she only dozed off for a few minutes. The engine of the snowmobile was still warm.

When she woke, there was no sign of her husband. She screamed for him into the blackness. She wished for him on the falling stars. She roared through the night on her snowmobile steed, searching every dark corner of those woods for her love.

And she could not find him.

Nor could the police.

Nor could the town.

Iris's loss rhymed with mine.

And in the days that followed, we buried Iris's grief in pillow forts and pizza and movie marathons and my father's voice telling story after story.

The first day after her father disappeared, Iris

did not shed a tear. She did not believe. She laughed loud and ate extra helpings and insisted there was nothing to fear.

The second day after her father disappeared, Iris did not cry. She did not speak at all. She watched the windows, waiting for word from her mother.

The third day after her father disappeared, Iris did not get out of our pillow fort.

My father sank down to his knees just outside the fort. He lit a candle. I'll never forget the way the light of the candle inside our fort flickered through the sheets and onto the walls. He lit a candle, and he knelt down and he spoke to Iris.

I never knew what he said.

But I'll never forget glimpsing her through the entry of our pillow and sheet castle to see her finally break, fling her arms around my father, see him scoop her up, and let her cry into his shoulder. And I'll never forget when Rosa and I crawled inside and threw our arms around her, too, as if, somehow, our three sets of arms, our three beating hearts, could save Iris from the chasm opening under her.

Her grief was like a Wil E. Coyote cartoon. She'd gone over the cliff. Only she didn't know it. And there in that pillow fort, she finally knew. And she dropped right out of the sky.

That night, Iris did not know how much she was losing. She knew only about her father. She did not know that the mother she had known. The free, warm, caring mother, the thoughtful, considerate, cookie-baking mother, the smart, funny, cartoon-loving mother, would vanish, too.

All her mother's warmth frosted into cold. All her mother's care and thought and cookie-baking, all her quips and cartoons and hugs froze in the wake of her husband's absence. From that night, she thought only of her husband's fate. Everything else was merely duty.

She did her duty, of course. She went through the motions. But she performed those duties as a husk. It was a husk that tucked her daughter in, and it was a husk that made sure she'd done her homework. It was a husk that picked her up from school, and it was a husk that came to parent-teacher conferences. It was a husk that pretended to care when the only thing that her mother would come alive for was the possibility of her husband.

The cold had set right in. From that first night, her mother's blonde hair had started to gray, as had her blue eyes. And even her skin. The cold seemed to get into her bones. And whenever we went to her house, it was always very cold, the heat barely on hot enough to keep the winter away.

She did her duty, and that was all. And she seemed to wait, always, to die.

And sometimes, it seemed as if Iris was waiting for the same.

But secretly, her mother obsessed. Obsessed over what had happened to her husband.

The police said he froze to death out there in the

woods, that his remains were probably buried along with the people of Morton's.

But Iris's mother didn't believe it. Not for a second.

It was only later that we found that out, though. At the time, she said nothing at all to Iris. To anyone.

And Iris was left with only the musketeers and my father for a real family.

It was only in our arms that she could find warmth.

And it was in those days, I think, that the bond between the three musketeers was sealed even tighter.

CHAPTER 4

IRIS WAS THE one that came with the charm bracelets. After the loss of Iris's father, her mother could not speak in words. She could not speak in held hands or hugs. She could not speak at the dinner table. She could not do any of the things a mother ought to do.

But she could give gifts.

She could give gestures.

She could give the things that didn't require words, that could slide out from her secret places in a language all its own. She could be present. She could give gifts. And no more.

And it was this language that Iris learned in those days.

And so Iris gathered them for us.

Three silver chains for our wrists.

And a first charm for each of us.

A sword in silver.

To represent the three musketeers.

She presented them on one of our pancake breakfasts. My father was a great aficionado of the pancakes. He could make them thin and thick. He could make them with chocolate chips or blueberries. He could drench them in strawberries or syrup. He could speak his loves in syrups and fruits and flours and wheats.

And we three musketeers would gather round our kitchen table and delight in all the flavors of my father's love.

It was my father that read us the book and my father that showed us the film.

So it was appropriate that it was my father who made us the pancakes the day that she brought them.

It was a sleepover night. We had lots of those. She didn't say a word about her gift all through the night. We'd stayed up late. And we'd talked about the things we always talked about. Ghost towns and long lost parents.

"My dad won't say anything," I'd said. "I don't know if she left or she vanished or…"

"I'm so sorry," Rosa said.

"My mother's the same," Iris said. "I know she's trying to find out what happened to him. But she won't tell me anything. She won't talk about him at all."

We had talked about this so many times, and yet, every time we did, we pretended like it was the first time. As if somehow, in the repetition of the facts, we'd find something new, something that we needed.

"You don't know anything at all about that night?" I asked for the million and first time.

"Well," Iris said. "Just that they'd gone out to watch the stars fall and that she fell asleep for just a second and that, after that, he was gone. But there was no...no sign he was leaving or anything. He hadn't taken anything with him."

And the silence that followed that was the same silence that always followed that.

"My mom was the same," I would say after a suitably respectful silence. "Car in the garage. Clothes in the closet. Just gone. During a meteor shower."

A silence would follow that.

"My mom disappeared during a meteor shower," I would say.

"My dad disappeared during a meteor shower," Iris would say.

"Morton vanished in a meteor shower," I would finish.

And we'd sit with that. We'd sit with it and sit with it until the conversation turned into cartoons and pop stars.

And on the morning after a night like that, Iris brought out the charm bracelets with the sword charms.

And over blueberry and chocolate chip and strawberry pancakes, we raised our wrists.

And Iris proclaimed, "One for all."

"And all for one," Rosa and I echoed.

And the silver of the swords glinted at our wrists.

And the taste of pancakes on our tongues, a night of stories told and stories heard on our hearts, we swore ourselves each to the other.

But, also, from those nights, I knew. I was not alone. I knew. My mother was not the only fatality of these mountains.

So from a very young age, I knew. The only answers I would get would have to come from the ghost town itself. But I also knew that I'd have to wait for that particular mission. It was a rite of passage, but it was dangerous.

As I'd discovered when I was thirteen years old.

When I snuck out of the house at midnight. And I wandered into swirling snow in the direction of a thing that glowed so brightly in my mind.

My father had fallen asleep early that night while we watched an old movie. The black and white of the tv screen flickered across his face, and as it did, my eyes drifted toward the window. To the line of towering trees. And in my mind, there was a glow.

In my mind, something beckoned.

I grabbed my walkie-talkie.

"Musketeers, this is Porthos, out," I said.

"This is Athos, out," came Iris's voice.

"This is Aramis, out," came Rosa's voice.

"It's time," I said. "It's time to go to Morton."

And minutes later, the three of us stood in front of the line of trees, armed with flashlights, armored in winter coats and snow boots, ready for adventure.

"I don't know about this," Iris said.

"Come on, where's your sense of adventure?" I asked.

"Still in bed," Iris said.

"But don't you understand?" I asked. "It's not just my mom. It's your father, too. We've looked and looked, and nobody has the answers."

"And you think that a ghost town in the middle of the night is going to have answers?" Iris asked.

"Yes," I said.

I met Iris's eyes. Those crystal blue irises shadowed by loss and midnight. "Yes," I repeated. "Whatever happened to your dad, it happened to my mom, and it happened to the people of Morton."

"My dad froze to death," Iris said. "So did your mom. Hypo-hypothermia can set in in ten minutes in w-weather like this. Death can occur in under an hour. That's all there is to the story."

"You don't believe that," I said. "I know you don't."

Iris closed her eyes. "I don't," she whispered.

"Then we have to do something," I said.

"Can't we just…go to the library again?" Iris asked.

"We've been to the library," I said.

"Maybe a different library? We could get your dad to take us to the one in Marquette. They have a really great section on…on local environments."

I crossed my arms and raised an eyebrow.

"There's only one place we haven't looked," I said. And I pointed into the woods.

Iris and Rosa followed my pointing finger and stared into the shadows. Everything was darkness, but in my mind, the glow, the glow of answers called my name.

"Rosa, what do you think?" Iris asked.

Both of us turned to look at Rosa. Her skin was very pale, and it seemed to glow in the moonlight, gathering light like the snow. "I don't know," she said. "I…I think it's dangerous. I think what Maeve says makes sense. But…it shouldn't be up to me. I'm not…I'm not missing a parent." There was a bitterness in her voice at that, as if she wished that she, too, was down a parent under mysterious circumstances. "This is up to you and Iris."

And so I turned back to Iris.

And, God forgive me, I raised an eyebrow, crossed my arms, and said, "I triple dog dare you."

A glint appeared in Iris's eye then. A glint that I knew would. A glint that I had put there knowingly and with intent. Because nothing got Iris going like a triple dog dare. "Fine," Iris said. "Let's do this."

"One for all," I said.

"And all for one," they echoed.

And so the three of us turned and marched into the dark.

And the dark closed in around us.

I'd seen the maps. I'd studied them. I thought… how hard could it be? Morton was a straight line from Dackett on all the maps. So…we'd walk in a straight line, and we'd find it.

At first, this seemed to go to plan.

We came to the ridge where, once upon a time, I had made snow angels with my mother. The three of us stood on that ridge and gazed out upon a perfect, starlit night, and that great ocean of trees. And our blood pulsed with adventure and wonder.

I led them down the path into the forest, and still, all seemed to go well.

We reached the creek, where stones formed a little bridge for small feet. We laughed as we skipped from stone to stone and crossed one more threshold into the forest.

And so we went on.

And it was here that everything went wrong.

We went on walking in a straight line, and it became very clear, very fast that what looked like a few minutes following a straight line on a map was not, in fact, that simple.

And that was one of the darkest nights of all the nights of the three musketeers. But it wasn't the darkest. No, unfortunately, that night still lay in our futures.

We wandered through the woods for a long, long

time. The end of my nose went numb first. And then the tips of my fingers inside my gloves inside my coat pockets. Then the tips of my toes inside their two pairs of socks inside their snow boots. And the numbness only spread from there.

It was luck alone that we didn't die. Well, luck and my father.

The night was dark and cold and the hour was late. And one tree was no different from the others.

Iris was the first to collapse into the snow. I turned to tell her to get up when Rosa collapsed by her side. "H-hypothermia can set in in t-ten minutes in this w-weather," she said, repeating her warning from earlier in the night, her voice as wispy as the white plumes of breath she expelled as she spoke.

I took a deep breath. And the air, so cold, made my lungs feel all the tighter, my heart beat all the harder.

And at last, I knelt in the snow and knew that we all would die.

The cold crept closer.

And in that moment, as I prepared to give myself to the blackness and the ice, there came the rev of an engine, the bright flash of lights, and then, suddenly, the feeling of wind and snow on my face.

Through the blur of my exhaustion and the cold that night, three things are seared into my memory.

The first…

When I opened my eyes, my dad sat in front of us, astride snowmobile, armored in a snowsuit much thicker than ours, helmed by thick hats and goggles.

My dad rushed forward, slipping off his coat and wrapping it around me. He lifted his goggles so I could see his face. The look of relief on my father's face when he wrapped his arms around me left me with no way to doubt my father's love. The pain that I caused him was too abundant, the warmth of his arms too strong, to ever doubt. Not then. And not for a moment since.

My dad took all of us on his snowmobile. We were small enough to do that then.

He brought us back to our house, where Iris's mom and Rosa's mom were waiting.

The second seared memory is the look on Iris's mother's face when she turned from her daughter to me. It was a look that blazed and seared. It was a look so hot that I'd never have imagined it possible to come from Iris's ghost of a mother. In that moment, she hated me. In that moment, I thought she would never forgive me. Not ever.

Iris had been forbidden from spending time with me after that, but Iris's mother could not stay angry for long and could not attend to such things for long either. She was, except for that one shining moment of hate, a prisoner of her near total apathy.

The third memory is the expression on Rosa's mother's face. I'd almost never met Rosa's mother. She was a tall, imperious, beautiful sort of a woman. A woman whose dark hair fell in waves about her pale face. And as she surveyed the scene, I saw no relief, nor fear, nor anger in her eyes. There was only a sparkling interest as she examined me and the others. Her hand lay upon a glinting diamond at her throat-set within a silver shooting star, and I'll never forget how the glint of that diamond looked so like the glint of her eyes. And that's how she's always been for me since. A shining ice sculpture of a woman. Our own Milady de Winter.

But I never have known what her expression that night meant.

But I think, I think, that in some secret part of her, she liked me, and she liked her daughter. And maybe some secret part of her longed for the girlhood and the adventures that she had lost within her frozen soul.

She grounded Rosa for a week, but she never forbade her spending time with me.

On the walkie talkie that night, when my bones had finally warmed, and I lay curled up under the blankets, I called for them.

"This is Porthos," I said. "Athos, Aramis, are you there?"

"Athos is here," Iris said.

"Aramis is here," Rosa said.

"I'm so sorry," I said. "I should have known we weren't ready. I should have known. I'm so sorry. Are you both alright?"

There was a pause.

"Grounded for a week," Rosa said.

And then I asked the question that I almost never asked, that I never dared ask because I feared the answer. "She didn't hurt you, did she?"

"No," Rosa said.

"And you, Iris, are you alright?"

When Iris responded, her voice was strange. "Yes," she said. "Yes, I'm alright. My mother, she… I'm grounded indefinitely. But I never…I never knew she cared. And she told me things…things about my father. Don't be sorry, Maeve. You were right. My mother says she thinks that there's something out there in the woods that took him, that took your mom, too."

"Did she say what?"

"No," she said. "She doesn't know what happened, but she hasn't given up. Science doesn't know…*quite* everything *yet*. Maeve, I think you were right. There are answers down there, but we aren't…"

"Ready," I said for her.

"Right," Iris said.

"Well, then, we'll get ready, and we'll try again," I said. "When the time is right."

"When the time is right," Iris echoed.

We waited for a long time, but there was no third echo. "Rosa?" I asked.

"When the time is right," she said, her voice very soft.

And so we resolved to wait. And try again.

We should have learned to call our hubris hubris long before we did.

I guess I should only say I. I should have learned to call my hubris hubris, and the others should have learned not to follow.

But I didn't learn, and they didn't learn.

But we did promise our parents not to go looking for that town again for a very long time. And, of course, all three of us crossed our fingers behind our backs.

To ourselves, we promised we would wait until we were older, wiser, stronger. We would study the maps and learn the paths so that we would not need saving.

Senior year, we'd go.

Like everybody else.

It would be a rite of passage for us, too, then.

Our answers could wait that long.

CHAPTER 5

IT WAS LATE February of senior year, and Dackett was buried in a perpetual snowfall. The sun had not been seen for months. The sky was a chrysalis of ice. Even the clouds were frozen.

Dackett had performed its yearly transformation into a snowglobe. Dackett always felt like that in the winter. Nestled in its valley, all year long Dackett resembled nothing so much as the perfect American town. With its cobblestone streets and the steeple of the church that rose to the highest point in town. With its main street of brightly painted stores and its neighborhoods full of families and their pets. With its baseball diamonds and its playgrounds and its old brick schoolhouses. But when winter came, the town underwent a metamorphosis.

When the sky froze over and the snow settled

down for a long nap on roofs and on tree limbs, when the town filled up with snowmen and snow castles and ice forts. When the lake froze over, and its surface became the canvas for ice skaters' blades. When the first snow fell, that perfect American town became something more than perfect. It became a fantasy town. The kind that could only exist in a snowglobe for its perfection made it too beautiful to be real.

But when you walked down Main Street at night, and you saw the glow of candles and shop lights, you couldn't help but wonder if somehow you'd stumbled into the snowglobe that lives atop every grandma's mantle come Christmas.

But for all its old-fashioned perfection, Dackett was a modern town with all the amenities of the modern world. The movie theater may have looked like something from the 1950s, but it showed all the latest films. The teenagers danced and drank to the latest pop songs. And our homes had televisions and VHS players.

And there was something else about the people of Dackett. They had money. Now, I don't mean that everyone was rich. But if you looked at the poorest of the poor in Dackett, those families had houses, food on the table, and a television.

All in all, for all its isolation, Dackett was a good place to grow up.

People in Dackett also knew how to handle the winter. There was an understanding that sometimes, roads would just not be drivable. And that was never an excuse for the closure of businesses or schools. It was just an excuse to get out the snowmobile. Everyone in town had one.

That morning, though, was a car morning, not a snowmobile morning.

For my sixteenth birthday, my father had passed me his old Subaru and bought himself a brand new one. He'd had the Subaru for the majority of my childhood. The gray interior stank always of long lost happy meals and that sour mildew smell of seats constantly soaked by snow.

There are moments in life that rewrite all the others. Ever since it happened, that reality has fascinated me. How something that can take up so small a portion of your life. Something that could last only hours or minutes or even seconds could rewrite your entire future, could dive into your identity and re-shape it.

When I got up that Friday, I had no idea that by that time tomorrow, no part of my life would be the same.

That morning, in the hours leading up to the moments that changed everything, Rosa sat in my front seat, and Iris sat in the back. Rosa leaned her head against the window, staring out at the passing landscape of snow-clad houses. Her dark hair clung to the glass, and her hazel eyes looked as crystalled over as the sky.

In the back, Iris was absorbed in Stephen

Hawking's *A Brief History of Time*, a look of furrowed concentration on her freckled face, her pale blonde hair forming curtains around her cheeks, as she continually worked the silver cross pendant she wore around her neck through her fingers.

"Every Rose Has Its Own Thorns" was just finishing on the radio when I pulled into our Friday morning breakfast spot.

Friday morning, my friends and I had a ritual.

I would drive the three of us from where we all lived on Everard Avenue to the local diner off Main Street, the one right next to the statue of Bob Dackett, where we would pig out on pancakes before school. That meal was the last normal meal I ever had. The last sliver of normalcy before it all came crashing down.

We sat around our usual booth in the corner of the diner. The walls were made of exposed wood, and the ceiling of exposed rafters. It was the sort of place where the air tasted of maple syrup, and your shoes stuck to the floor. We always felt so sick afterward, but we never even considered ending the ritual.

I sat in the corner of the booth with a stack of chocolate chip pancakes before me. To my left, sat Iris with her blueberry pancakes, and to my right, sat Rosa with her strawberry pancakes.

Iris pushed back her pale, straw hair as she took her first bite. For a wisp of a girl, Iris could put away more pancakes than me or Rosa. Her pale green eyes reminded me of springtime in the mountains (usually late May or early June) when the grass emerged green and triumphant and the flowers began to bloom on the tree (after nearly nine solid months in hiding).

Rosa, on my other side, dug into her strawberry pancakes, pushing her glasses up on her nose as she did so. Rosa's hair was dark and curly, and usually she kept it pulled back behind her head. Today it was free. I liked it that way. It made her look softer, warmer, more herself. She wore glasses that I always thought were way too large for her face. But I also had come to see those glasses as part of her face.

"So Rosa," Iris said, "any new correspondence from your pen pal?"

I looked over at Rosa. Any mention of her pen pal caused her face to turn beet red without fail. She did not let me down. Her face was the red of the strawberries on her pancakes. Rosa and Robert had been pen pals for over a decade when they'd met at a church camp. They both belonged to some very strange denomination of church that Rosa always refused to talk about but that required a frankly exorbitant amount of her time.

"Well," Rosa said. "Yes. Robert's asked me if I want to come for a visit sometime."

Iris and I grinned. "And…?" I asked.

"And… well… I told him I'd think about it," she said.

Iris smiled gently, but I feigned banging my forehead against the sticky table. "The answer is yes," I said. "The answer is a most definite yes."

"Well, I have to ask my parents," she said. At the mention of her parents, some of the blood drained from her strawberry cheeks. "Obviously, Robert's parents are part of our church and everything, but..."

I let out a long sigh and shook my head. "They'll say yes," I said, although I didn't know that. None of us knew anything when it came to Rosa's parents. All we knew was the shadows that crept into her eyes whenever she mentioned them. But I plowed on, trying to keep the tone light. "Don't string this guy along. He is so in love with you."

Rosa frowned. "I don't know," she said very quietly, her face now passing from strawberry red into the violet of Iris' blueberry pancakes. "He… we're probably just friends. You know how these things go."

I shook my head again, laughing. "Yes, I do, and he's head over heels for you," I said.

Iris gave Rosa an encouraging smile. Rosa was so smart about everything and everyone, but when it came to her own life, she was absolutely hopeless. "He does write you, um, rather a lot of letters," she said. Iris was the queen of understatement. By "rather a lot of letters" what she meant was that he'd written Rosa a new letter nearly every day of every week ever since her family came back from their visit last summer.

Rosa shook her head. "I just don't know," she said and took a giant bite of her strawberry pancakes. "And I think my mother will say no. You know I have this, um, big thing coming up."

Iris and I exchanged a look. Rosa had been making strange allusions to this big thing at her church every few days over the last several months. "When is that big thing?" Iris asked, her voice soft.

"Oh, any time now," Rosa said, staring into her pancakes. "I…my mother's not very happy with me. It's…it's a rite of passage in our church, and I…" Here, she choked, her cheeks flushing even redder. When pressed too hard, when her cheeks matched her strawberries so perfectly, it was always time to drop it.

Iris took pity on her and turned to me.

"Any word from Marquette?" she asked.

The mention of Marquette meant graduation. The thought of graduation was bittersweet to me in those days. All my life I'd dreamed of leaving Dackett, Michigan, exchanging the small town for the bigger city of Marquette. But now that time was approaching, I'd found myself becoming strangely sentimental about Dackett.

I looked down at my Friday stack of chocolate chip pancakes, and I felt that nauseating twinge of premature homesickness. Of all the people in our senior class, I never imagined I would be the one infected by such appalling sentimentality. Shoving the feeling aside, I took a giant bite of the pancakes before shaking my head.

"I have not heard," I said. My anxiety about that was a whole other emotional bottle of worms I had no desire to partake in over pancakes. "How about you?"

"Full ride," she said. She took a demure (and triumphant) bite of her pancakes.

"Congratulations!" I said. "That's amazing!"

"Perseverance," said Iris, pointing a piece of fork-speared pancake at us, "is the key. I'm sure you'll get the same letter soon."

I laughed, trying to switch the conversation into less stressful waters. "Speaking of perseverance," I said, "I do not think I'm going to do well on the Calculus test today. I could not focus last night."

Rosa rolled her eyes. "You always say that, and you always do well," she said.

"Not as well as you," I said.

But Iris reached out and patted my hand. "You'll be fine," she said. "We're here."

A look of confusion passed over Rosa's face.

Iris turned to her. "Today is February the 24th," Iris said.

A look of horrified understanding dawned on Rosa's face. "Oh gosh, I'm so sorry," she stammered. "I forgot the date."

"No, no, it's fine," I said. "We'd better get going to school, or we'll be late."

"Right," Rosa said. "Surrender your spare

change. I'll go up and pay."

Iris and I passed her the money, and she promptly scooted out of the booth and scurried over to the cash register to pay.

I started to scoot out of the booth, but Iris put a hand on my arm to stop me. She turned to her purse and pulled out a little box.

"My mother always says that it's worth honoring the hard days," she said. As she spoke, the cross pendant around her neck glinted with the rosy light of the sunrise outside our window. For all her mother's faults, she always remembered birthdays and had a knack for giving gifts at just the right time, even if, from day to day, she barely knew her daughter existed. "I know you don't like to be reminded of your mother, but I picked this up for you ages ago and thought I'd give you this on a day when you couldn't help but remember her."

The box in front of me was wrapped in a deep violet wrapping paper decorated with tiny golden stars. I unwrapped it carefully, a smile tugging at my lips.

Underneath the wrapping paper, I found a simple wooden box.

"Open it," she said.

I opened the lid of the box. Inside, I found a metal charm shaped like a shooting star.

"I know how your mother always loved shooting stars," she said.

"It's beautiful," I said. "Help me put it on."

She took the shooting star as I held out the wrist on which I wore the charm bracelet, the sisters of which adorned both Rosa and Iris' wrists. Through the years, we'd added many different charms after those initial swords.

Each of us had some of the same charms, but Iris loved to buy Rosa and I charms for special moments. Iris had given Rosa a fist to represent the moment that Rosa had punched her bully in the face. I'd received a ribbon to denote my status last year as the number one female cross country runner in Michigan. And we all had the dragon that represented the summer we'd all three stood up to Rachel Mathers and Kurt Blonton and effectively ended their reign of terror over the children of Dackett Elementary.

And, of course, no charm bracelet would be complete in Dackett without a tiny little replica of Bob Dackett.

Rosa arrived back at the table as Iris finished adding the shooting star.

For a frozen moment, she stared down at the charm on the bracelet, a strange, haunted look on her face. Her hand went to her own chest for a second where hung a barren silver chain, and then she smiled.

"It's lovely," she said.

Iris reached for her Diet Coke and lifted it.

Knowing what she wanted, I lifted my own, and Rosa reached over and grabbed hers.

"To the three musketeers," Iris said. "One for all."

"And all for one," Rosa and I echoed. We clinked glasses, and we drained our sodas down to the last drop.

And with that, the three of us got up and walked out of the diner, the bells above the door jingling as we left. I looked up at the ten foot tall statue of Bob Dackett with his big smile and his broad shoulders.

I waved to him as I always did. This was part of the ritual, too. "Morning, Bob," I said.

"Morning, Bob," Iris said.

"Morning, Bob," Rosa said.

And we headed out to the car to face what at that moment I assumed would be a day of nothing more strenuous than a Calculus test.

I don't think I've ever been more wrong about anything in my life.

CHAPTER 6

WHEN I STARTED the car, "Every Rose Has Its Thorn" was playing once again on the radio. Rosa went back to staring out the window, and Iris picked up her copy of Hawking from where she'd left it propped open on the seat beside her.

When the song finished playing, the DJ started talking.

"And don't forget, citizens of sunny Dackett, that tonight's the night of the big meteor shower," he said with a croon. "Weathermen predict that we'll see quite the display in the wee hours of tomorrow morning just before the big blizzard rolls into town, and friends, it's gonna be a big one. But before it comes in, astronomers say this should be the biggest lights display seen since the 1881 display that coincided with the disappearance of our local ghost town. And, in honor of the stars, here's one from America's biggest. Madonna…"

I turned off the radio and turned to look at Rosa and Iris.

It was a sign.

The anniversary of my mother's leaving.

The shooting star charm.

A sky of shooting stars just like the day that Morton disappeared.

"Tonight," I said. "It has to be tonight."

Rosa turned away from the window, a gleam sparking in her brown eyes. From the back, Iris lifted her eyes from Hawking. That same gleam sparked in hers.

"Are you sure?" Iris asked.

"Did you not hear the radio man?" I asked. "It's going to be the biggest meteor shower since the original one back in 1881. We have to go."

"I don't know," Rosa said. "I stayed up sort of late studying."

"And I was up late practicing for my recital," said Iris. "It's only two months away now, and I'm nowhere near ready."

"And what about the blizzard?" Rosa added.

"Oh, blizzard-shmizzard," I said. "We'll be there and back again before the first snow falls."

"I don't know," Iris said. "During the blizzard of '78, the wind moved at a rate of between fifty and seventy miles per hour and windchill got down to thirty below."

"We won't be out late enough to have to deal with that," I said. Come on, you guys. This is it. We've been waiting all our lives for this. The big adventure. The last adventure in Dackett before we go off to college. And tonight is perfect. Can you imagine? With the meteors falling, it'll be just like it was back in 1881. It'll be like going back in time and seeing exactly what all the residents of Morton saw just before the end! How can we not go?" I met Iris's eyes. "It's a night just like the ones my mom and your dad…" Iris closed her eyes.

"How shall we do it?" asked Iris after a long pause.

"Same plan as always," I said. "We sneak out at midnight and meet at the Oak behind my house. I've had my Adventure Bag packed for this since the first day of school. I'm ready."

"One last adventure for the three musketeers," Rosa murmured.

"One for all," I said.

"And all for one," they echoed.

And I'd never felt so warm and so alive and so electric on a February the 24th.

Normally, I am not a minder of school. In fact, to be perfectly honest, I liked school. I liked the people. I liked the teachers. I liked the classes. I liked the sports. So while I may talk a big game about rule breakage, it wasn't coming from a place of hatred of the school. It was simply born from a spirit of fun.

But that day, I minded school.

That day, I couldn't focus on my Calculus test, and I couldn't comprehend what Hamlet was trying to articulate about nunneries.

All I could think about was that night. All I could think of was the cold wind in my lungs and a sky emblazoned by flaming stars. All I could think about was the roar of adventure in my blood. It was all that I could hear. All that I could feel. All that I could think.

I had not read the Stephen Hawking book that Iris was trudging through, but I had my own theories about time. By now, I thought I knew how time played us mere mortals. It would drag by all day long. Every tick of the clock would appear to be a second but somehow it would contain minutes.

But it would be worth it. Because when I snuck out that night. When we ventured out into the woods. Then time would cease to operate. There would be no seconds at all. There would be no minutes. There would simply be Adventure. And when it was over, we would re-enter the timestream wherever time bid. But for the space of our adventure, we would be free, unmoored. Time would hold us like we were balloons on the ends of thin, but very long, ribbons. As if time was just a child, and we were free to kiss the wind.

And it would be glorious.

Or so I thought. I didn't know then that Time was not a careful, cautious child like Rosa that held onto her balloons with clenched fingers. No. Time was like me. I'd never received a balloon whose ribbon didn't slip through my fingers. Time was the child that let her balloon go and watched it sail away, away, away, into oblivion. Time was the child that let it go on purpose. Simply for the joy of watching that balloon disappear.

But I didn't know any of that then.

All I knew was that an adventure waited for me when the clock struck midnight.

But until then, I had to get through a day that was exponentially, infinitely longer than any other school day I'd ever experienced.

But got through it, I did.

The sound of the bell at the end of the day sent my heartbeat thudding into a run, even though there were still nearly ten hours to go before the adventure could begin. And those hours would be long. At least at school, there were distractions.

When I got home that night, I could focus on absolutely nothing. Somehow, I managed to slog through homework and make dinner in time for Dad to get home.

Dinner with Dad would be the only true obstacle standing between me and adventure.

No matter what I did, Dad always knew.

Dad often worked late during the week. He was an architect, and he was working on a new office building in Marquette. It was a long drive. But he always made it in time for dinner. Since I'd been in middle school, we traded off dinner responsibilities. Neither of us were wonderful cooks, exactly, but neither of us were terrible either.

When Dad arrived home that night, I had not prepared anything special. If I'd done that, he'd know. I'd made the usual spaghetti and meatballs.

We never did anything special on February 24th. We just always made sure we were home. That we were together. We always pretended like everything was normal, but it never was. And I'm ashamed to say that I knew I could work that to my advantage. So while I prepared to make the conversation at dinner as normal as possible, I knew I could use the anniversary to mask the reality of what I was hiding.

"How was your day, Mavers?" he asked.

"Oh, it was fine," I said. "Kind of boring. Are you going to get up and watch the meteor shower tonight?"

Dad shrugged. "I doubt it," he said. "It's pretty cloudy with the blizzard supposed to roll in. I don't think we'll be able to see much."

"Probably not," I said. "How goes the new building?"

Dad shrugged again. "Business as usual," he said. "Aaron is getting frustrated with the pace. But with the cold…"

"It's not safe to work," I said, shaking my head. "He must understand that."

"In theory," he said. "But he's not a Yoopie. He and all the other corporate types don't really know what it's like up here."

"Well," I said, "you should get a few days of decent weather, right? Thirties anyway."

"It's supposed to get really cold tonight, actually," he said. "If you get up for the meteor shower, make sure you bundle up before you go outside."

"Yeah, yeah," I said, kicking him under the table. "Worry wort."

"I'm not joking," he said. "A teenager at the university in Marquette died two weekends ago from exposure. Poor kid had too much to drink at his first frat party and didn't put a coat on when he walked back to his dorm. He blacked out on the way back and never woke up."

"That's awful," I said.

"Yes, it is," he said.

"I'll bundle up," I said. "If I can get myself out of bed. I'm tired tonight."

Again, the thought of college had brought the rush of unwanted, premature homesickness as the red sauce of my spaghetti stretched out before me into all the nights and all the dinners of my childhood in which me and Dad had sat at this table and eaten this same spaghetti. Canned tomato sauce and box spaghetti were not worth my nostalgia.

The conversation petered out for a moment. "Hey," Dad said as he rubbed the red from his lips with a napkin. I looked up from my plate.

"Yeah?" I asked.

"There's… something I want to talk to you

about," he said.

My heart heeded this cue and began to thunder. This was never a good sign. "Yeah?" I repeated. "What, um, about?"

"Your mom," he said.

"But that's against the rules," I said. "Not on February the 24th. Never on February the 24th. That's our rule."

"You know better than anyone that some rules are made to be broken," he said. "And besides, there are some things that can only be said on… February the 24th."

There was a pallor to my father's face as he said it. I stared into the mountain sky blue of my father's eyes, and I thought I'd never seen those eyes look so brave.

"What… what is it?" I asked.

Dad took a deep breath and began playing with his watch, clicking the buttons on the side over and over again, spinning the wheel until I was sure the watch would never tell the right time again.

"I lied to you," he said. "Well, I didn't exactly lie. I just didn't… tell the truth about… today."

"I am aware," I said. "You never told me anything."

"She didn't leave," he said.

"What?" I asked.

"She didn't just leave," he said. "She didn't choose to go. I just let you think that."

I took a deep breath. I never thought we would

actually have this conversation. "Go on," I said.

He shook his head. "It was wrong, but I was… grieving. And for a long time, I convinced myself that's what happened. For a long time, I was lying to myself. But it's been thirteen years now. And I think it's time I faced it."

"Okay," I said.

My father took a deep breath. "It was a night like this one. Very cold. There was going to be a meteor shower, and you know how your mom loved that kind of thing."

I touched my finger to the star charm Iris had given me earlier that day. "I know," I said.

"She got up in the middle of the night to go see the lights," he said. "And she never came back. She… she must have died of exposure just like that kid in Marquette. Only… only we never found her."

Dad's face was pale as the snow outside. And in his eyes, I could see the emptiness. That big wide mountain sky. The loneliness. Not the peace kind. The kind that drove you mad.

"I'm sorry, Dad," I said.

"For years, I… I told myself that she… that she left me," he said. "But I knew that wasn't true. Everyone knew it wasn't. I…" He took a deep breath. "I went a little crazy that night. Saw things that weren't there. It took me a while to get my head straight. I'm sorry it took me so long to tell you."

I looked at my Dad, and I felt about a hundred thousand emotions all at once. And all the while, that whole conversation, one of the most important conversations of my life, I could feel the minutes stuffed into the seconds, could feel the long drag of all the words. My skin still itched with it, and now here he was, rewriting history. But was he rewriting it, at all? After all, after all, I'd always thought she didn't choose to leave. He said he'd seen things that weren't really there. What if he'd seen the ones that took her?

I wished I could go back. I wished I could go back and tell him it was alright. That I understood. But, to be honest, I didn't understand. In that moment, all I really knew was that I'd been…I guess he hadn't lied exactly, but that was how it felt.

"I wish that you'd told me," I said.

"What would have been the point?" he asked. He met my eyes. Those mountain skies, lonely and mad and solid and unyielding.

And I closed my eyes. Five hours to go. In five hours, I could leave. In five hours, I could run. In five hours, I would have the big adventure I'd spent my entire life dreaming of. And in five months, in five months, I'd be gone to college.

"Okay," I said.

"Okay?" he asked.

"Okay," I said. "I'm just… I'm going to need a minute."

"Okay," he said.

"Or maybe a few hours," I said.

"Okay," he said.

"Potentially a few days," I said.

"Okay," he said again.

The conversation faded into silence at that point. I finished my spaghetti. Dad finished his spaghetti. We lingered a little too long over the red stain where once there had been spaghetti. We'd done this too many times to need to talk. In silence, I washed and Dad dried. The only sound was the running water and the clink of plates as Dad put them away.

Then we sat in the living room and watched a new episode of *Star Trek*. Just like we did every Friday night. As much as I loved the adventures aboard the Starship Enterprise, I couldn't tell you a thing about that episode. At that point, I don't think any of my senses were functioning properly. They were somewhere ahead, somewhere a few hours hence. My eyes and my ears and my brain had time traveled to the future and left the rest of me behind, sitting on that couch waiting for time to pass so I could join them.

They were most certainly not in this room. They were most certainly not on the information my father had just given me. They were most certainly not on my father as he sat with glazed eyes and stared unseeing at the screen.

I knew he saw as much of that episode as I did.

But we both sat there because it was tradition. Because I was Maeve, and he was Dad, and that is what we did because we loved each other.

At last, the episode ended, and my father went to

bed. He kissed me on the top of my head before he went. That much I do remember. It was a casual kiss. The kind he placed on the top of my head every single day of my childhood. If I'd known that kiss would be the last, maybe I would have paused to feel it for what it meant.

"Love you, Mavers," he said lightly.

This was the part where I said "Love you, too, Dadders." I'd said it like clockwork every night of my life. Every night since I knew the words.

But I couldn't get them out.

Or, maybe, it isn't that I couldn't. Maybe it's that I wouldn't.

He waited for a second at the foot of the stairs, listening for it. When it didn't come, I watched his shoulders slump. And he started up the stairs.

I waited until I heard him close his bedroom door.

Then I stood up, crossed the living room to my own bedroom on the ground floor. I brushed my teeth. I put on my pajamas. I got in bed. And I lay there. And I waited for the light up display of my alarm clock to reach the witching hour.

And I didn't think of my mother or of the vision of her death that my father had laid out.

I didn't think of her laying in bed one night thirteen years ago.

I didn't think of how excited she must have been to see the meteor shower.

I didn't imagine her getting out of bed.

I didn't think of her putting on her coat but maybe not her full snow suit and slipping out the glass door to the porch.

I didn't think of her walking out into the woods and finding a good place to watch the lights.

I didn't think of her on the ridge.

I didn't think of her shivering.

I didn't think of her fingers turning blue.

I didn't think of the end of her nose going numb.

I didn't think of her at all.

I stared at the red numbers in the darkness of my bedroom. Sometimes, I turned on my side and stared out through the window. The blinds were open, and through them I could see the slow glow of snowfall, as a thousand little white lights descended on the trees and upon our house.

And after what felt like a thousand years, it finally reached midnight.

Chapter 7

THE MOMENT THAT the 11:59 became 12:00, I leaped from my bed. In seconds, I had changed into my snow suit, laying at the ready over the chair by my desk. As Dad had asked, I bundled up.

I threw my Adventure Bag, with its contents of extra flash lights, first aid, food, and water, on my back, and I rushed to the glass door of my room. Before I opened it, though, I removed from the pack the black flash light. I'd put in fresh batteries the moment I'd gotten home. Flashlight in hand, I was ready.

I lifted the old walkie talkie to my lips.

"This is Porthos," I said. "I'm ready."

"This is Athos," came Iris's voice. "I'm ready, too."

A pause.

"Aramis," came Rosa's voice. "I...I'm ready, also."

"I'll see you out there," I said with a grin.

Cautious and slow, I pushed open the glass door and stepped out onto the porch that wrapped around the house.

My boots crunched in the fresh snow that piled on the porch. I breathed in the sharp cold of the night air. It tasted like adventure.

I gazed up at the sky. The perpetually frozen clouds lay thick, but through some cracks in our snowglobe of a town, I could just see the twinkling of a star or two. But there was no sign of meteors.

Walking to the wooden railing of the porch, I gazed down at the steep slope that led from the line of houses into the woods. The snow glittered with reflected light. Down below, I could see two shapes already huddled beneath the large oak tree at the edge of my property. I waved down at the figures, and they waved back. The three musketeers were nothing if not punctual.

I ran down the wooden steps, sparing one last glance at the house and at my father's window. It was dark. He had to be asleep. If all went well tonight, I remember thinking, he would never know I left. I remember thinking how light I felt as I practically flew down the slope to my friends. I remember thinking this is the part where time stops. This is the part where adventure starts.

Sometimes, when I think about that day, when I

think about that night, I can't help but imagine how it could have gone differently. I pretend that when I reach my friends, I tell them, "Hey, I think we'll get a better view of the meteor shower from here. Let's do the ghost town another night." There have been many nights when I have so carefully, so painstakingly assembled a fantasy of how that night could have gone. When I lay awake all night long playing and replaying my improved version of events. Such thought cycles help no one at all.

When I reached Rosa and Iris there at the base of the oak, I didn't suggest watching the meteor shower from home. Nor did I suggest watching a movie or catching up on sleep or telling them I felt ill.

"Ready for an adventure?" I asked instead, lighting my flashlight.

By my pale flashlight gleam, I saw the smiles of my two friends.

"Never readier," said Rosa, lighting her own.

"I'm always ready," said Iris, lighting her flashlight. "Although, we need to make this fast. They're saying that this could be the worst one since White Hurricane of 1913. Wind gusts reached speeds of up to ninety miles per hour and over two hundred fifty people died and…"

I put out my flashlight like a sword, cutting Iris off. Rosa and Iris shone their flashlights so that the three beams met like the swords of the three musketeers.

"One for all," I said.

"And all for one," they echoed.

And so it was that the three of us, the three musketeers, turned to the woods and began our walk through the forest, the triple beam of our flashlights illuminating the path before us.

I should have feared the woods at night. The parents of Dackett never fail to teach the children of Dackett two things before they can so much as walk and talk: the fear of the Dackett woods and the skills necessary to survive them.

Somehow, my father, for all his efforts, had never managed to teach me the first. Rosa and Iris were afraid. I could tell from the way they stuck to my sides, from the extra pallor of their faces, the quick lash of their flashlight beams every time a twig broke nearby.

But me, I felt no fear.

The woods were my home. They wouldn't hurt me. They couldn't hurt me. Not anymore. I wasn't a child any longer. I'd spent all the years since our last attempt getting ready for tonight. Nothing could go wrong.

And so I led Rosa and Iris through the trees on paths long buried by snow. The fresh snowfall had filled in whatever tracks might have been left recently by snowmobiles or men.

"Are you sure you know the way?" Rosa asked.

"Oh, yes," I said. "I know the way."

And I did. After our first catastrophic attempt,

I'd poured over maps of the woods. And although I'd never gone all the way to the abandoned town, the paths to get there were branded on my memory. And they still are.

"It just seems like we've been walking for a long time," Rosa said.

I snorted. "We've barely been walking five minutes," I said.

"Oh," Rosa said, falling silent at that.

"We're almost to the ridge," I said.

"Oh," she repeated. "I forgot about the ridge."

Iris laughed. It came out high-pitched and unnatural. And it died in her throat as a deer ran through the beam of our flashlights.

"There it is," I said, stepping between the trees and arriving at a place where a sudden drop-off had sent more than one snowmobiler to an early grave. And where, once upon a time, my mother and I had laid inside snow angels and watched a star fall.

As we stepped out from among the trees, I gazed up at the stars. The sky was clearer here. It wasn't just a star or two that twinkled now from above, but a dozen or two dozen stars. And they burned bright.

There was not a cloud in the sky. There was no indication that a blizzard was due for arrival in mere hours.

And here is another place where I often try to stop my story. In my head, I imagine myself saying, "What a wonderful view! Let's just stop here and watch the meteor shower!"

But I didn't say that. I didn't even think it.

Behind me, Rosa and Iris had both stopped and turned their faces up to the stars. The illumination of the night sky reflected silver on their faces. And I remember taking the time to treasure that moment. To take a photograph in my mind of the way my two best friends, age eighteen, just before heading off to college, looked when the starlight fell from the sky and the snowlight rose from the ground and from the trees and cast them both as angels. I memorized their faces. Wide and open and full of awe and perhaps, a trace of fear. I memorized the furrowed freckles on Iris' brow and the fog from Rosa's breath that obscured her glasses. And I remember the sound of our laughter and its echoes as she rubbed that fog away.

But I didn't say the words that I wished I'd said. I didn't even think them.

Instead, I said, "Come on. Let's keep moving. We've still got a long walk."

And so we hurried on alongside the ridge.

The path ran along the ridge before following the downward slope of the cliff into the deeper parts of the forest. The ridge was the demarcation line between forest that was little more than a wooded part of Dackett and the woods that no one could really claim to own.

We reached the bottom of the ridge, and we plunged back into the woods. The trees here grew thick and close. Very little starlight managed to pierce the roof of branch and pine, even when, in winter, many of the trees stood barren and empty.

Only our three flashlights cut a path before us in the dark.

This time of winter, snow completely obscured the path. But I knew my way. I could have guided the three of us through these woods without the flashlights.

Rosa and Iris pressed to each side of me, their arms brushing against mine as we walked. Neither of them spoke.

"So which theory are you going with?" I asked. My intent was to break the tension with conversation. My choice of topic may not have been the best for my purpose.

"Aliens," Iris answered. "I think it was aliens. Did you know that the earliest recorded UFO sighting in America was in 1939? The Puritan governor of Massachusetts Bay said that these men on this boat saw a flaming light in the sky, and when the light faded, they were a mile upstream. They must have come on the meteors and moved the people in Morton, just like the men in Massachusetts."

"What do you think, Rosa?" I asked.

"Gods," she said quietly.

"Gods?" I asked. This was a theory I had not heard before.

"Maybe they came from the stars," she said. "And maybe they needed a sacrifice."

"What for?" I asked. "Why do gods always need

a sacrifice?"

"So that they can grant the people's wishes," she said.

"Right," I said. "And why did they need to… eat an entire town of people?"

"Sometimes, even the gods get hungry?" Iris suggested.

"Because sometimes a big wish takes a big sacrifice," she said.

I cast my light on Rosa's pallid face. "That's creepy," I said.

She shrugged and adjusted her glasses.

The conversation fell off for a time. "Maybe they just left," I said. "Maybe they just got sick of the world. Maybe they didn't want the railroad. Maybe they just went off into the woods and… started over."

"No way," said Rosa.

"Not a chance," said Iris.

"The Dacketts would never have left Bob," said Rosa.

"Maybe the Dacketts weren't as nice as we always thought," I argued.

"Ridiculous," said Rosa.

"Absurd," said Iris.

"You never know," I said with a shrug, ducking under a low hanging branch.

"I wonder if there's anything interesting left for us to find," Iris said.

"The authorities probably gathered all the

interesting stuff up," Rosa said.

"Yeah, I heard that all the good stuff was gone," I said. "The houses are all pretty much completely empty."

"That's too bad," Iris said. "But there wouldn't be much to find anyway. With as much time and exposure to the elements that things have had up here, not much could survive."

"Tragic," I said mournfully.

At that point, we came to a little creek that wound its quiet way through the woods. In the summer, this creek bubbled merrily. I'd loved to play in it as a kid. There were rocks located at the perfect spots across the creek for jumping from stone to stone and alighting on the opposite bank.

But now, the creek was frozen over. I tested the ice with my foot. Should it break, the water was too shallow to rise above my boots. The ice seemed firm, but I hesitated, looking for the old stepping stones. It would be more fun that way.

As a seven year old, that first stone had been the furthest. I had to jump to reach it, and half the time, I wound up in the creek bed. But now, I had merely to take a step. My feet barely fit on the stone now, and for a second, I thought I'd slip off.

But I got my balance and stepped onto the next stone. This stone could only accommodate one of my feet, so with the other I reached out and stepped onto the bank on the other side.

Rosa followed in my footsteps, and Iris followed

in hers, laughing as she reached us. "We haven't done that in years," she said.

"Too bad," I said. "That was fun. I had forgotten all about doing that."

"Me, too," Rosa said.

I frowned as I led them forward, deeper into the woods. How many other relics and rites of my childhood had I simply forgotten about? How much had simply slid away unnoticed into the dregs of memory? When I left Dackett for Marquette in a few months time, what would happen to all of those buried treasures of the past? Would some part of me remember? Or would only the trees recall?

We walked for several more minutes in silence.

"How long is it supposed to take us to get there?" asked Iris.

"About an hour's hike," I said, "in ideal weather. We seem to be making good time, though."

My dad had been right about the cold. I was glad that I'd taken his advice and bundled up. The end of my nose had begun to go numb. Rosa and Iris were even more bundled up than I was, but Iris shivered as we reached a bend in the path.

I could understand how that Marquette kid had died in this cold. And the further out we went on a night like this, the more danger we were in. When I heard the chatter of Rosa's teeth right after Iris' shiver, it really did occur to me to turn around. For the first time all night, I actually considered abandoning the mission.

But I didn't say a word.

I just kept on going.

It wasn't the cold that got us in the end. But it could have been the cold that saved us if I'd only listened to that nagging voice of concern for my friends.

Somewhere far off, an owl hooted.

And on we walked, deeper and deeper into the cold night.

What was I thinking about as we walked through the night? I'm not sure I was thinking of anything but the path and what lay at the end. Sometimes, I'd laid awake dreaming that I'd be the one that discovered the secret of the ghost town, that after all these years, it would be me to uncover the truth. I guess that was why I had to go that night of all nights.

So I suppose that was what I thought of. Of the glory that I would find there. I was so sure. I was so sure that the secrets would spill themselves out for me.

The funniest thing of all is that I was right.

Chapter 8

Just as the ridge marked the line between the civilized woods and the woods proper, there was another line of demarcation. The line that I was never to cross. The line between the woods proper and the wilderness. It was a line that my father had always taught me to respect, a line I'd always been told never to cross. And it was somewhere past that line that we would find the ghost town we sought.

The line between came in the form of an old fence. The fence was little more than ten or twelve rotted wood posts set up at intervals amid the trees. According to my father, there used to be people that lived out in these woods, but that hadn't been for a hundred years. It was them that had left the fence behind when they'd gone.

When we came to the fence, I stopped.

This was the boundary of my childhood made manifest in the world. To cross it was to cross a symbolic (and literal) boundary into the realm of adulthood. And for all my hatred of boundaries and my determination to see rules undone, the idea of crossing this particular fence struck me down with yet another case of homesickness.

I saw myself as a little kid standing there with my dad. I saw Dad put a hand on one of the fence posts and use the other to gesture out into the woods beyond.

"Beyond this post, the woods are wilderness," I could hear him say. "You never go beyond this post unless you never want to come back. Am I clear?"

And I could see it through the eye of memory. My wild-haired, scrape-kneed childhood self nodding up at my father with a flame in her eye that told everyone with eyes to see that she would one day cross that post and come back.

"And here we are," I said to Rosa and Iris.

"We're there?" asked Iris doubtfully.

"No, no," I said. "This is the line. I've never been past this fence. Beyond that, I'll be relying on maps."

"How reassuring," Rosa said.

"To adventure," I murmured, and, with a thud of the heart, I stepped over what remained of the horizontal slats of my childhood and into the dark unknown of my future. I wish I never crossed that fence.

The woods had long been dark, but now they grew even darker as I walked.

"Wait," Rosa said, shining her light off to our left. "Is that a house?"

"There used to be people who lived out here," I explained as Rosa's light traced the ruins of a log cabin, the roof of which had long since caved in.

"Should we check it out?" Iris asked.

I shrugged. "I don't think there will be much there," I said, "but it seems a shame not to."

The ruin in question stood only yards away, so I led the way toward the dilapidated cabin.

"Was this part of the town at one point?" Rosa asked.

"We're still a long way out from the town," I said. "My dad said that when Morton was around, there were people who would live out in the woods and come to Morton for supplies and church and the rest. But when Morton went, the people who lived out here ended up dying out or leaving within a few years."

The door of the cabin had long since rotted off its hinges. It lay beside the doorway now, and snow blew through the opening.

I stepped inside, shining my light over what remained of what was once someone's home. The wooden beams of the ceiling lay broken in rotted pieces over the majority of the cabin. One long piece of timber skewered a badly carved wooden table, which now rested on only one of its legs.

Beyond the table, I saw the remnants of a bed beneath the roofing.

Shining the light over the walls, I saw shelves containing broken plates and cups, along with leaves and pine cones. Cabinets built into the wall remained intact along the Dackett side of the house, and Iris rooted through these. Rosa knelt at the foot of the bed where an old hope chest lay. She struggled with its lid until I heard a snap. When the lid popped open, I joined her to look down at a faded patchwork quilt, woven of many faded colors.

"Look at this," Iris said from beside us. She reached down and pulled a little journal from the chest. It had been tucked underneath the quilt where its edge had only just poked out.

"It can't have lasted this long, can it?" I asked, turning to face her.

Holding her light with one hand, Iris shone it down on the leather cover. "The chest and the blanket would have protected it from water damage," she said, her voice quiet. "Paper stored at thirty to forty percent relative humidity can last hundreds of years."

Rosa and I shone our own lights down on it. I reached out and opened it to a page that was so old that nothing was visible but dark smudges. I reached over and turned one page after another until at last, I found something.

There was no good way to describe the drawing. In the middle of the book, this page was the most protected from time. And on that lone page at the book's center, there was the barest ghost of a drawing. It looked like a kind of cocoon. Almost like that of a caterpillar. But the artist had drawn lines emerging from the cocoon as if to indicate that light came from it, or perhaps movement.

There was something about the shape of the cocoon, too, that seemed odd. That seemed too close to the shape of a human being.

At the bottom of the drawing, there was a single word.

"Aster," I whispered.

"I think those are buildings," Iris said, pointing to the mass of smudged shapes that constituted the background of the drawing. Now that she said it, I could make out hard lines and what could almost be a sign with words above a door.

"It's Morton," I whispered. "It has to be. Maybe whoever lived here saw what happened that day and drew it."

Rosa cleared her throat. "You're saying that the town was swallowed up in… what… cocoons?" she said. "Whoever lived here must have heard the stories that crazy miner told and decided to draw them."

"Okay, okay," I said. "Fair point. Maybe this was the crazy miner's house. Or maybe it really… "

"Everyone has their theories," Rosa said, cutting me off. "We have our theories, and so would the people of a hundred years ago. This is just somebody's theory. That's all."

"I guess you're right," I murmured.

Iris closed the notebook carefully and returned it to where she'd found it inside of the old wooden cabinet. She gave the cover a quick pat before closing the cabinet door.

"We should keep going," I said. "We aren't too far now I don't think. Just another mile down the path."

Rosa and Iris groaned. "Another mile?" Rosa said.

"And we have to go all the way back," Iris said. "I do not think this was the three musketeers' best idea. That blizzard…"

"Hey now, if all the other seniors can do this, so can we," I said.

Rosa and Iris rolled their eyes and followed me out of the ruined cabin and back into the cold completeness of the night.

We walked in our own footsteps back to the place where the stick lay still planted in snow.

And we pushed on.

One more mile, I told myself. That was all that stood between us and the greatest mystery we'd ever experienced. Just one more mile.

"Did you hear that?" Iris hissed.

Iris froze. I turned around and shone my light on their frightened faces. "I didn't hear a thing," I said.

"I was sure I heard something," Iris said, pointing off to our left.

I shone the light to the left, but there was nothing but trees. I strained my ears. The sound of the wind in the trees. The creak and groan of old limbs. The crunch of the snow beneath my feet. The occasional crack of branches nearby as animals moved in the woods around us. And then, somewhere far off, I heard it.

And I laughed.

"It's a snowmobile," I said. "Someone's just out for a nighttime ride. Yeesh. You should see your faces."

Iris and Rosa's shoulders lowered in relief, but their brows were still knotted.

"Come on," I said. "I think… I think we're almost there."

Iris snorted. "You've been saying that for the last hour," she said.

"No, no," I said. "Do you see how the land is sloping up? We're on Morton Hill. On the other side, we… well, we should get our first look at Morton."

Rosa and Iris's eyes widened at that. And suddenly, just like that, it was real.

And yet, even then, there was still time. Even then, we could still have turned back. Even to that moment, just on the other side of the hill, I return often in the middle of the night. In the silent whirring of my unsleeping mind, how many times have I stood again on that side of the hill screaming at the girls to turn around? To run back home as fast as they could?

As many times as there were comets in the sky later that night. Over and over and over.

But I just smiled, and there was a familiar light of adventure that twinkled in the eyes of my two friends. And we three musketeers continued on up Morton Hill. Every step bringing us closer to disaster. To our last adventure.

CHAPTER 9

IT WAS JUST as I thought. When we reached the top of the hill, we got our first look at the ghost town of Morton Valley.

In some ways, Morton was not dissimilar to Dackett. Both towns nestled in valleys next to lakes. Both towns were surrounded by endless wilderness.

In another world, I supposed that Morton would have been Dackett. In another world, this could have been my home.

If you look at Dackett from the hills above it, it always twinkles. It always winks.

But looking down at Morton, there was no twinkling of light. There was no wink.

After the encounter with the ruined cabin in the woods, I'd half expected to find nothing at all left of the old city. Just a series of ruined cabins.

But Morton was never just a cabin in the woods.

The town, as seen from above, looked much as it might have the day that Bob Dackett came back to town from his starcrossed supplies run.

Up here on the hilltop, I could see the big wide open sky. The clouds were gone now. And the stars blazed so bright they took my breath away. They blazed like light shone through ice. Still, they hung in place up above the world. But one could feel the coming of their descent. The air vibrated with it.

The silver light from the stars and the moon cast a ghostly pallor over the dead town.

From here, I could see the bones of the town, its houses and its shops, its stables and its schools. And in the middle of it all, I could see the high spire of the church still reaching upwards to God even in death.

Here and there, as I gazed, I came to find signs of the passage of time. A roof caved in. A house devoured. But overall, the town was a corpse that rotted slowly, preserved by the unending bone deep ice.

"Wow," murmured Iris.

"Creepy," said Rosa.

And just then, just as I was about to keep walking, I thought I saw, but I could never be sure, a twinkling of light from the spire of the church. It was there. And then it was gone.

"Come on," I grinned.

And I broke into a run. I ran down the hill in the

direction of the town, my feet accelerating with the effects of gravity. I broke through old cobwebs and charged through green branches laden with snow. Behind me, I could hear Rosa and Iris running. Iris breaking into a laugh. And then I realized I was laughing, too. And the sound of our laughter rose upward amidst the trees and broke through into the heavens.

And then, all at once, we came out from the trees and found ourselves standing on the main street through the town of Morton.

The three of us just stood there at the start of that road, gazing at the two parallel rows of houses, at the unmarred surface of the snow before us.

"Just think," I said. "Over a hundred years ago, this is the exact road on which good old Bob Dackett, our illustrious town founder, rode with his horse and cart only to discover his entire world vanished." I turned to them and grinned. "Isn't it grand?"

I led the way forward, shining my flashlight over the houses on either side of the road. At one time, I think these houses would have been considered very well-to-do. They rose to two stories, and they were made of firm wood that had stood strong against the ravages of a century without upkeep.

"It's incredible," I said.

"Everything is so well preserved," Rosa murmured.

It wasn't that the town had escaped the last

century completely unscathed. There were broken windows aplenty, and the unbroken ones had gone completely opaque. A few doors hung off hinges, and nearly all the paint had long since chipped away. And in one house that we passed, we saw a great hole, as if some giant had taken a bite out of the front of the house. But overall, the buildings were intact.

Iris and Rosa walked on either side of me as we continued down the road. Our footprints in the snow were the only interruptions in the perfect white glow. The snow lay thick on the road and on the roofs of the buildings. Long icicles hung down from the eaves of houses. A tree that stood at the next street corner was encased totally in a cocoon of ice.

I shivered. It was getting colder.

There was very little need of our flashlights now with the sky so bright and the snow reflecting back that light. The windows of the houses looked down on us with glazed eyes.

We were alone. I knew we were alone. And yet, there was a feeling of something else here. I felt that familiar goosebump sensation that something or someone watched. And yet, there could be no one.

I glanced at Rosa and Iris. On both of their faces, I saw the same uneasy expression that I felt.

"How far are we from the town square?" asked Iris as we walked through a four way stop.

"Not far," I said. "It's a straight shot down this

road. I think only two more blocks now."

We didn't talk about going inside any of these houses. Everyone knew that there were certain places you had to go while in Morton. The locations from the story. The Dackett house. The church. Nowhere else mattered.

I'd heard that some kids tried going down into the mines once in the 50s. They'd found the mines completely stopped up. Now, no one bothered looking there. Besides, the mines weren't part of the town proper. It wasn't the mines where people were taken. It was the town.

"One more block," I murmured.

Somewhere far off, I could hear the rev of that lone snowmobile out on his midnight mission.

With every step, I felt that I was walking into a certainty. I'd dreamed of this night all my life, and now that I was here, the very edges of my vision had the blur of a dream. But the sharp cold of the air in my lungs reminded me that this was real.

And then we came to the town square.

The eye was drawn first to the church. The old time religion had been the pulse beat of the old town, just as it remained the pulse beat of Dackett. They'd built the church to be strong as their faiths. And the fact that it stood nearly unblemished a century later testified to that. The white paint was chipped out of reckoning of course. The glass windows were blind. But the clock tower spire with its bells still soared as high above the town as ever it did. There was no sign now of the light I thought I'd seen.

The rest of the square looked just as I'd always imagined it from all the stories. There was the Dacket General Store. The windows of the store were broken, but the door still stood. The carved wooden sign above the door still read General Store. And it occurred to me then that this could have been the store drawn in the background from the drawing in the cabin in the woods.

The other buildings were all there. There was the police station and the jail, the town hall and the post office. And all of them stood more or less as I'd imagined them. The town hall had received time's most brutal treatment. Longer and wider and larger than the church, though not quite as high, the town hall's construction had not been built to last. Little remained of the hall but rubble and frame. A skeleton of a town government as mortal as every other.

"Where first?" Rosa asked.

"I really want to see the church," Iris said, her eyes on the bell tower with its grasping spire.

I glanced from the church to the Dacketts. "Let's save the church," I said. "Make it the finale. Let's check out the Dackett house first."

Turning the beams of our flashlights to the old General Store, where the Dacketts had both lived and worked, we approached the opening where an old door still remained. Under the glow of our flashlights, I thought the house might once have been painted yellow.

I walked up to the door and took a deep breath.

"Do we knock?" Iris whispered.

I gave a choked laugh at that, and I reached out and pulled open the handle. The hinges of the door creaked angrily, but the door opened all the same.

We shone our lights past the door and into the shop beyond, illuminating strange shapes and long shadows.

And with that, we stepped into the house.

Iris and Rosa stepped behind me.

I lifted my flashlight and shone it over the counters. It was as I imagined it would be. The long rows of shelves behind the counter, all empty now. There was nothing left to buy here but snow and leaves and cobwebs.

A smell of wet decay hung on the air, and, for all its appearance of wholeness, I thought the place seemed fragile.

I imagined all the ghosts of what might once have sat on these shelves. I saw cans and carrots, cigars and clothes, candy and chicken and cloves and cucumbers and coal and calendars. There might have been salt and soap and silverware, flour and fabric and flowers, baking powder and baskets and board games.

Now, there was dust and dirt. Now, there were cobwebs and cracks. Now, there was snow and soot.

On the other side of the counter, I found the

kitchen door ajar next to the stairs that would lead up to the Dackett home.

Pushing myself up and over the counter, I made for the door.

Rosa coughed purposefully as she lifted the wooden board to join me on the other side.

"My way was more fun," I said.

I pushed the door open the rest of the way. A blackened fireplace where Mrs. Dackett might once have made meals gazed unseeing from across the room. Hooks on the walls now hung without their pots and pans. Cabinets on the walls that once stored plates lay empty now, the glass broken. The old kitchen table remained, though.

On that table, we found not half-eaten bowls of soup, but instead a crowd of empty bottles of Budweiser, candy wrappers, and empty fifths of cheap vodka and whiskey. The detritus of teenagers past and present.

"It seems disrespectful," Iris said, her eyes on the mess of a table.

"It is disrespectful," I agreed.

"On that line," Rosa said, "aren't we being disrespectful, too? This place doesn't belong to us. We're violating the privacy of the dead."

Iris looked to Rosa with a worried expression. "I hadn't thought of it that way," she murmured. "I... I think you're right. It's almost like being a grave robber."

"Hey now," I said. "Grave robbery is an essential

tool in the historian's toolbox. Without it, we wouldn't know a thing about Ancient Egypt. It's not like we're leaving garbage like those idiots did. Or doing any damage."

Iris shook her head, and I saw in her eyes, a familiar steel. "And how did grave robbing work out for the people that found King Tut's tomb? Lord Carnarvon and his half-brother died of blood poisoning. Sir Archibald Douglas-Reid died from some strange disease, and George Jay Gould died from a fever. Then there was Sir Bruce Ingram. He was just given stuff from the tomb, and his house burned down and *then* flooded after it was rebuilt. No, no, this isn't like going up on the roof of the school," Iris said. "It's one thing to go into the shop but to go into their homes. I won't do it."

"I triple…" I began, but then I stopped.

Something in her expression stopped me. Iris, at most times, was as passive as the wind. She floated along with whatever was going on around her. But once her conscience awoke, then she was more stubborn than I was. It was this part of her that bought charms for her musketeers and always remembered Little Tommy Wart Fingers birthday (and his actual name, which was always more than I could say).

"Okay," I said.

"I know I can't stop you from going," she said, "but I'll just wait in the shop."

"Are you coming, Rosa?" I asked.

Rosa looked from Iris to me and then to the staircase.

"We'll be quick," she said to Iris.

Iris gave a quick nod, pushed her pale hair behind her ear, and walked back in the direction of the shop. If I'd known that was the last time I'd ever see her, I would at least have watched her go.

But I didn't know. And by the time Iris had turned, I was already halfway up the steps, carefully testing each old wooden board before I put my weight down on it.

The stairs held, and I reached the second floor.

The second floor was smaller than I imagined and darker. The windows allowed in little light. The sitting room stood stripped of all furniture. On the wall, there were dark squares where pictures might have hung.

I walked to the windows that overlooked the town square, but you could see nothing through them but a dim glow. I thought it had to be from the snow.

Rosa walked carefully through the sitting room to the hall beyond.

She stood at the first of three doors and pushed it open as I approached.

Through the first two doors, we found nothing. Just empty rooms with dirty floors and broken windows. There was nothing left now to speak of what once was. Nothing but a feeling. A sorrow that seemed to lay thick about the very walls of the place.

The last room, I thought must be Bob's, but it was impossible to tell. Nothing was left. Not so much as a single chair. The room had been properly cleared out.

"What do you think happened to them?" I asked, more to myself than to Rosa.

But then Rosa spoke. And when I looked at her, her eyes were faraway. "Well," Rosa said. "I mean, maybe it's like I said before. Maybe they…these aster people…maybe they were like gods," she said. "Maybe they…took sacrifices to…to make a better world."

"What do you mean?" I asked.

"The Copper Rush barely lasted a couple years," Rosa said, running her fingers on the dust of the window pane. "A few years, and this town was dead anyway. But in its place, somehow, Dackett was born, and Dackett thrived. So maybe…maybe there's an exchange. A life or lives for more life. And the aster are just the…mediators."

I stared at her. "I guess that could…could make sense," I said.

"There's nothing up here," Rosa said. "Should we go back down?"

I walked back to the middle of the room, feeling thick on my skin the sorrow of the walls. "Yeah," I said. "I'm right behind you."

Rosa moved off in the direction of the stairs, and I cast one last look around the room, turning a circle as I did. But there was nothing here. Just a couple leaves, some dirt, and a lot of dust.

But just then, something glinted on the windowsill.

Pulled toward the glint, I went to the window.

There on the dusty, snowy wood, was what looked like a broken charm. It lay in three shattered pieces, each one covered in rust. When I moved them together, they formed a little silver star, much like the one on my charm bracelet, much like the one that hung around Mrs. A'Hearn's neck.

It was nothing. Just a leftover relic of a time long forgotten. Maybe this was Mary Lynne's room, and it belonged to a necklace. Maybe Bob Dackett had a thing for shooting stars. Maybe some teenager or other had left it here.

I gazed for one more moment at that tri-shattered star.

It was nothing.

I should have known. I did know. All those years, all those teenagers, all those authorities, local, state, and federal, there was no way that anything would be left for a couple teenage girls a hundred years later, especially not here.

Disappointed and deflated, I turned and started across the living room.

As I reached the stairs, I heard Rosa shout from below. "Maeve! Maeve, get down here!"

Giving no heed to caution, I ran down the steps into the store part of the building.

I found Rosa standing by herself on the customer side of the shop. Her face was pale.

"Where's Iris?" I said as I ran toward her.

"I don't know," she said. "She's gone."

"Don't be silly," I said. "She's probably just outside."

I ran past Rosa and charged out into the night.

Up in the sky, the comets had begun to fall.

They fell like burning raindrops. They fell like fire on the world. They fell like tears of blood. They fell trailing their clouds of immortal glory. They fell like they might have fallen a hundred and eight years ago. They fell like they did when they took the town. And so they fell. And so Iris was gone.

The square was empty. The glazed eyes of the windows bore down on us from all around, lit in ghastly shades by the colors in the sky. The collapsed town hall looked like a devil's grin of broken teeth. The spire of the church rose high and uncaring, reaching out in answer to the falling stars. The police station brooded from its corner, unfazed by the display in the sky, and the post office watched in parody of its long abandoned rounds.

And Iris was not there.

"Iris wouldn't just leave," said Rosa. "What she says she'll do, she does. She said she'd stay right there, she said… if she's gone…"

"I know, I know," I said.

"What do we do?" Rosa asked.

"I don't know," I said, beginning to turn on the

spot just like Bob Dackett had done all those years ago.

"You always know what to do," she said. "Come on, what do we do?"

"I don't… I don't know!" I yelled back. "I just don't know."

I fell to my knees. I felt the cold of the snow even through my snowpants. "I don't know," I whispered.

"Iris!" Rosa yelled.

I forced myself back to my feet. "Iris!" I screamed.

We yelled her name until we were hoarse. Until we couldn't yell anymore. But there was no sign of Iris. She was simply gone.

And then there was a sound like the roar of a lion, and when I turned to face it, I was blinded by light.

CHAPTER 10

THE LIGHT WAS the headlight of the snowmobile. It roared into the town square, its lights flashing across my eyes. Rosa reached out and grabbed my hand with a squeeze.

The roar of the engine died, and I heard two feet crunch upon the snow. I blinked my eyes, trying to banish the stars that obscured my vision. A large, dark outline of a person stood before me. He pulled off his helmet.

"Dad?" I asked.

His cheeks were red. And although I could not see his eyes behind his snow goggles, I felt sure that they would be red, too. The veins in his temples would be throbbing.

"Well," he said, "at least you bundled up."

And then he hugged me.

"Where's Iris?" he asked as he let me go.

"I… I don't know," I said. "She was here. She… she said she'd wait in the Dackett store when we went up. But when we got back down, she was gone."

"What do you mean? Gone?" he asked.

"I mean gone," I said. "She wasn't anywhere. Not in the house. Not out here."

"Did you check out back?"

"No, but we've been shouting for her…"

My dad didn't waste another second. He let go of me and ran between the houses to their back. I charged after him, Rosa close behind. The meteors went on falling above us.

But as we rounded the corner of the house, it was as I expected. There was no sign of Iris. Just an old stump where Mr. Dackett might once have split wood.

My father scanned the area quickly, and then he hurtled through the back door into the Dackett house. We followed after him. He made a quick search of the downstairs, and then he ran up the steps.

Rosa and I watched from the vacant sitting room as he checked every room.

"Where else might she go?" he asked as he came out of Mary Lynne's bedroom.

"I don't know," I said.

"She always said she wanted to see the church," Rosa said. I thought then of the light I'd seen from

Morton Hill. Could there be someone else in this town? Could there be someone who didn't like teenage girls breaking into ancient houses?

"Then let's go to church," he said.

And so we followed after my father as we ran back down the steps. He charged through the store and back out into the square. Our feet crunched against the snow as we barreled toward the Morton Valley Church.

My father paused as he reached the great wooden double doors but only long enough to seize one of the old brass handles and pull.

There was a sound almost like a popping, and there was a rush of fleeing air as the door opened. Snow skittered into the darkness beyond.

And the three of us pointed our flashlights into the dark.

My father led the way into the church.

The church was the first building so far that had not been ransacked. A century's worth of authorities and teenagers must have had enough respect for that church with its towering spire not to disrespect what remained within.

A line of simple wooden pews led up to the pulpit. On the pews, old prayer books and hymnals sat yellowing into eternity. The floor of the church lay covered in a thick layer of dust. The cross that hung above the baptistry at the other end of the church cast a heavy shadow across the floor. Silver and gold light from the sky poured themselves through high windows behind the cross, giving the plain wood of the cross the glow of a halo.

It was a simple kind of a church.

Nothing fancy or ornate. But in this light. After all these years, it contained infinities.

"Iris?" Rosa whispered.

"Iris, sweetheart, are you here?" my father called, louder.

"Iris, get your butt out here!" I yelled.

My father and Rosa both glared at me. "What?" I shrugged.

Each of us started toward the pulpit. Rosa went along the left side of the church on one side of the pews, my father walked down the center aisle, and I took the right hand side of the church. Our footsteps echoed and clanged against the high ceiling.

I bent down and checked beneath every pew as if Iris might have suddenly reverted to a child playing a particularly cruel game of hide and seek.

When I reached the end of the church, I stepped up onto the wooden stage and walked to its back. I gazed down into the baptistry. It was empty.

I looked up and shook my head at Rosa and at my father.

"She's not here," I said.

My father said nothing for a long time.

His eyes lingered on the windows above my head. They glowed gold with the light of the falling stars outside.

As I looked once more around the church, something glinted on the ground just a few feet away.

I knelt down and found a little silver cross at the end of a silver necklace. Momentarily, it had caught the fiery glow of falling stars.

I lifted it up to the light. Once more, it glowed with the reflection of the fire in the sky. All three of us stared, hypnotized for a moment, at the dangling, flashing cross.

"Iris was here," I whispered.

"The bell tower," my father said. "She must have gone up to the bell tower."

And with those three words, I tensed. I thought again of the light I'd seen coming from that tower high on Morton Hill.

Pocketing the cross, my body started walking in the direction of the tower before I made a decision to move.

Dad and I reached the door at the same time. It was an unobtrusive little door that I'd missed when we'd first come in. It clung to the shadows next to the main entrance, wreathed in cobwebs and dust.

I reached out for the handle and pulled. The door opened with a terrible squeak.

Inside, a long staircase wound upward into darkness. The stairs turned at right angles along each side of the tower.

I started forward, but my dad put out his hand. "Let me go first, test the stairs," he muttered. I hung back, knowing that in these matters, I could not out-stubborn my dad. If I argued, we would only waste time.

He started up the stairs, testing his weight against each groaning step, just as I'd done in the Dackett house. The stairs held his weight, and he moved up them quickly. I came just behind, always on the step just below him.

Rosa hung back at the bottom of the stairs, her hands clutching the rails of the stairs, watching us with eyes made wide by her glasses.

"Come on," I said. "Remember what happened last time someone waited at the bottom of the stairs."

Rosa's eyes widened, and she hurried after us.

And we proceeded up the creaking, groaning steps.

Dad came to the point where the stairs ended. He reached up into the dark and felt around. A second later, I felt a rush of cold air and silver light as he pushed open the trapdoor. He hauled himself up and through, and I pulled myself just behind him.

The old bell still sat solid and silent just as it had the day Bob Dackett found the people of Morton vanished.

Iris was not here. There was no one here.

Just a snow-strewn floor and a relic of a bell.

There were no footsteps in the snow. I saw no sign of the light I'd seen from the hilltop.

I walked to the edge of the tower and leaned against the chipped white of the old railing and looked out on the town.

The town of Morton stretched out below me. It was alight with the burning golds of the falling meteors. The whole town burned orange and gold and white in the icy snow. The light filled up the icicles on the eaves and the ice-cocooned trees until from here, the houses and the trees looked aflame. The whole frozen town burned.

It had told us nothing. It had been empty of everything. Everything but the ghost of a nightmare.

"I don't understand," I said as my dad made a round of the tower, staring out from every side of the tower, straining his eyes for any sign of Iris. If she were here, if she were outside, we would have seen her from here. With all that light, from all the way up here, there was no way we could miss her.

"Where is she? We were separated for literally like two minutes," I went on.

My father wasn't looking at me. His eyes, his face, his whole body danced in the light of the falling stars as he spoke. "I think *they* took her," he said.

"They?" I asked.

He looked down at me and frowned. "The same ones that took your mother," he said.

"You said she died of exposure," I said. "You said she…"

"I told you I thought I was crazy. I told you I

thought I saw things I didn't," he said. "But… but I think I wasn't ever crazy." He held me firm. One hand on each shoulder. And his eyes now were like the mountain sky again. But now his eyes, for all the lonely sadness, for all the fear, somehow contained peace, too. "She and I came down here," he said. "She was like you are. She liked adventure. We came down here, and she went into the church. And when I came after her, she was gone. I thought I… well. Anyway, there was a meteor shower that night. It must have been the light from that. But I thought I saw her disappear in a cocoon of light. And I thought I saw someone there in the shadows beyond her. But the second the light died, there was no one there."

I looked up at my father and shook my head. "You did see something, Dad," I said. "We found a drawing in a cabin in the woods. It was of someone disappearing in a cocoon of light. Isn't that what… isn't that what the crazy miner said? Isn't…"

"Stop," Dad said, suddenly freezing. "Where's Rosa?"

"Right behind me…I…" But she was not right behind me. She was not on the tower at all.

I felt it then. What Bob Dackett might have felt that day. The hammers bursting through his heart.

And then I did the same thing Bob Dackett did. I pushed it aside, and I went on.

I turned and opened the trapdoor.

Rosa was not at its base.

I dropped back through the trapdoor, my father just behind me. I walked faster down the steps now that we knew the way was secure. The stairs groaned and whined beneath our traipsing footsteps.

At the bottom of the steps, Rosa was not waiting.

Nor was she in the church.

Those hammers in my heart thundered all the harder.

We left the empty church then, shutting the door fast behind me.

I found Rosa standing in the middle of the square. Her eyes were on the stars. The lights of falling meteors made a golden filigree of the sky and of the square. We stood now not above the burning but in its midst. The golden light cast itself over her face, painting her with those same flames.

I ran across the court to Rosa. She slowly turned her gaze from the lights above us to me.

"Rosa, thank God you're still here," I said, throwing my arms around her.

Her teeth chattered, and tears streamed down both cheeks.

And then something happened.

The whole world got brighter.

I pulled back from Rosa. There was light, light all around me. I was in a cocoon of it. And Rosa gazed at me with sadness in her eyes but not fear.

"Rosa?"

"There's a blizzard coming, Maeve," she said.

"And it's going to kill lots of people. Worse than what Iris was telling us about the White Hurricane of 1913, and two hundred fifty people died in that one."

I stared at her. None of it made any sense at all.

"What you said before…"

"My family," she said.

"You're killing me," I whispered.

"I'm giving you to the Light," she said, tears streaming down her face. "To save the town."

"Don't," I said.

And Rosa closed her eyes. "It's *my* rite of passage," she whispered. "They said it's the right thing to do. They said it's what you'd want. To save the day."

"Did you take Iris?" I asked.

"My mother," she said. "Because I didn't take you. She's just going to keep taking people until I… it's to stop the blizzard…save the town…"

All these years. All these years of secrets. I thought that what Rosa hid about her family was, at best, a weird cult, and at worst, abuse. And maybe it was both. But this…alien beings. Gods. The aster. Who was she?

But I looked across at the girl I'd known all my life with her dark hair and her pale skin, and her eyes more terrified than I'd ever seen them. I knew exactly who she was. She was a three musketeer. She was warm nights by the fire, sleepovers stuffed with pizza and stories. She was laughter and tears. She was home.

"One for all," I said.

Rosa sobbed.

"And all for one," she said.

And the light stopped. The light died.

"Run," she whispered. "Run. Get out of Dackett. Go."

And it was at that moment that I realized that we were not alone.

All around us, in the windows, and in the doorways, on the roofs, there were shapes, figures. Each of these shapes shone with a silvery light. Each of them was a person and a star all at once.

And among them, I spotted one I knew.

At the top of the tower stood our very own Milady de Winter, Mrs. Sarabeth A'Hearn. She stood above us all, above all of those other shapes. And although she was far off and far away, I could see her face so well, as if her features were lit up by a brilliant light and carved from stone. Carved from ice. Her eyes flashed with a brilliant crystal blue darkness. And the light that she cast was like the light of a mirrorball. She was one of those meteors come to life.

At her throat, glinted her diamond shooting star necklace. The diamond now shone with light. And she stepped forward, her hands curving around the railings.

She lifted a hand.

And as she did, all those shapes began to move.

They all took a step forward.

"Run!" Rosa screamed.

I turned toward my father's snowmobile. Between it and me, a dozen of those silver shapes now blocked me. My father stood a few yards off from me, between me and the church, his eyes trained up above on Rosa's mother.

Between me and him, another half dozen shapes.

"Run!" Dad yelled. "I'll meet you at home!"

"Run!" Rosa yelled.

And so I ran.

As I did, the bells in the church spire began to toll.

Chapter 11

Bells that had not tolled for over a hundred years rang out as the stars fell from the sky.

The sound of the bells chased at my heels, driving me on faster and faster, even as those silver shapes lunged toward me.

One toll.

I darted between two of those shining figures, those figures who I would have mistaken for angels if I didn't know better.

Two tolls.

I ducked between three more, veering down an alley.

Three tolls.

And there were five of them on my heels.

Four. And I could see the end of Morton on the horizon.

With each ringing, with each echo of each ring, I raced harder and harder from that place.

I refused to look back or around. I refused to look at anything but the next point in the race.

It is a universal truth in life that eventually, no matter how great you are at something, you will always find someone better than you. No matter who you are. But at age eighteen, I'd yet to be beaten in a race. Back home, my room was full of ribbons and trophies. On my charm bracelet, there was the charm Iris had given me when I was declared the fastest girl in Michigan.

That night, I ran faster and harder than I'd ever run before and harder than I've ever run since.

I ran with all the fire of my soul.

First through the town with its leering shining army of the angelic monsters.

Then past the town's edge and into the woods.

I don't think I've ever felt so horrifyingly alive as I did as I ran those three miles. I felt every sharp, cold breath in my lungs. Every pump of my heart. Every rush of my blood. As I reached Morton Hill, I pumped harder, forced myself faster up that hill than I've ever taken a hill before.

As I reached its top, it began. One moment, the sky was clear. The next, the snow poured down in sheets nearly as thick as rains. The world turned white. The blizzard had arrived.

At the top of the hill, as the blizzard came down, I had one moment of hesitation.

I had one moment where I considered turning back.

Where I wondered if I was a coward for running and leaving Rosa and my father or whether I was right to run, right to survive and fight, rather than give into certain death?

I looked back. Like Orpheus and Lot's wife. And all I saw was a blaring white light through the great white fog of snow, and all I heard was one last toll of that great, old bell. And when I didn't turn to salt, I ran on.

Because that was the only thing I could do.

And the hammering went on inside my heart.

And I plunged down into the woods as the last echo of the last toll died on the howling wind. I heard every twig beneath my feet and every sigh through the trees. All of it entered and filtered through me.

I felt that night as if I was a part of the woods, and the woods were a part of me. I felt all the loneliness with its mad sorrow, and I felt, too, the great and total peace of that place. And above me and around me, the meteors painted the snow and the trees gold. And the world looked like it was aflame, a flame that the falling snow caught and reflected into the air itself was afire.

I ran and I ran and I ran.

Sometimes, through that great fog of whiteness, I thought I was not alone in the trees. Sometimes, I thought there were shapes there around me. Faces.

Faces of women and men and children. A face like Bob Dackett's. A face like my mother's. But when I would turn to look, there was only the blazing reflection from the sky.

I ran past the collapsed cabin in the woods, and I leaped over its fence. The fence that I never should have crossed. The fence that marked the line between wood and wild.

Around then, I thought I heard the rev of an engine, a snowmobile, and I allowed myself to hope. Allowed myself to imagine my father with Rosa behind him, zooming away to safety. They'd be waiting for me when we got home. We'd light a fire, and everything would be alright. And maybe, maybe Iris would be there, too. And my mother. And Iris's father. And…

I put on a burst of speed as I hurtled through those trees, up and down the hills and the embankments. But even as I did, the blizzard fought me. The wind grew harsher, stinging every exposed bit of skin.

My nose went numb first.

Then the tips of my fingers. And the tips of my toes.

And the numbness began to spread.

When I got to the creek, I didn't bother to jump from stone to stone. I simply jumped across in a single leap.

By the time that I reached the place where I thought the path that would take me up the ridge to the town part of the woods, I was tired, and if there was a path, it was buried in fresh snow.

I was more tired than I'd ever been. My legs hurt. My lungs hurt. Every part of me hurt. But I wasn't going to stop. I'd made good time, and I refused to lose any now. I'd run the greatest race of my life, and I would not relent. I would just keep going, path or no path.

I ran harder than ever up that slope, pushing myself through the uphill to the very top. Even as blizzard winds pushed back, and the snow hid the world from sight.

But when I reached the giant oak behind my house, I stopped.

Parked beside the house, I saw my father's snowmobile. He'd gotten away. He would be inside. He'd be with Rosa. And Iris. And everything would be alright.

I started forward.

The house was cast with the silver and gold lights from the deep purple sky. But from within the house, there came another light. A strange light that looked not quite silver and not quite gold. A light that was neither natural nor artificial.

I staggered up the slope to the deck. The cold had gotten into my blood by then. I shuddered and shivered with it as my blood pumped ice through my heart.

My legs felt like jello beneath me. They could barely lift me up each step.

When I reached the porch, I stared into the house.

The light came from the living room.

I pushed open the glass door that we always left unlocked.

And there, in the middle of the room, I found my father.

He was encased from feet to shoulders in a cocoon of light.

And beside him, there was Rosa's mother.

And as I threw open that door, his eyes saw me, and he opened his mouth.

And I knew that right then and there was my last chance to say what I'd tried to say all night.

"I love you, Dad," I shouted.

And in those mountain sky eyes, I thought I saw relief.

But before he could speak, the light devoured all that remained of my father.

There was a flash. I thought I saw her then. Rosa's mother. Our own Milady de Winter. An imperious smile on her beautiful face.

And then everything went dark.

When the stars had faded from my eyes, I gazed at a dark living room.

Outside, the meteors had ceased to fall.

And there was no sign of my father or of Rosa or of her mother.

I went to my knees.

"I love you, Dad," I sobbed. "I love you."

The winds stopped. And the snow stopped, too. The meteors were gone, and so was the blizzard.

I felt a hand on my shoulder. Rosa stood behind me, her face more pale and haunted than I'd ever seen it. Where I always thought the way her pale skin glowed with the snowlight made her look like a star, now I thought it made her look like a ghost.

"Go," Rosa said. "Go now. Get in your dad's Jeep and run. And don't ever come back. One for all."

"And all for one," I whispered, holding onto Iris's necklace in my pocket.

And so I ran.

CHAPTER 12

THE OFFICERS NEVER found Iris. And they never found my father.

The official explanation is that they must have gotten lost in the woods and died of exposure. Just like that poor college kid in Marquette.

But I don't think anyone really bought that.

The skies in the UP were just too wide for me after that. The madness was just too close.

Even if it hadn't been for Rosa's warning, I knew I'd have to leave.

I threw away everything. My track career, my scholarship, my last few months of classes, nearly everything I owned. And I ran.

It was Rosa's idea.

She had that pen pal. His name was Robert O'Malley. She said he'd asked her to come for a visit. She asked if I could come and stay with him and his family for a few days.

He said sure.

And so that was how I came to Torrance, Indiana and how Rosa followed only a few months after. She never spoke much about what happened to her in those months between my flight from Dackett and her arrival in Torrance.

But there were shadows in her eyes that hadn't been there before. And, from her arrival in the middle of the night at the O'Malley farm, dirty and tired and carrying only a single backpack, I knew that she'd run.

But when I saw her standing there, covered in dirt, her long hair now cropped close to her skull, deep circles under her eyes, on the doorstep illuminated by the spotlight of the porch light on that early summer night, she smiled. And I smiled.

"All for one," I said.

"And one for all," she said, and she threw her arms around me.

And we hugged and felt again in each other's arms, the flicker of my father's fireplace, the shadows of his carved figures dancing on the walls, the echo of stomachs full of pizza and throats sore from laughter, the presence of our third musketeer, and the man that was the only real parent any of us had ever had.

We hugged, and we were home.

Neither of us ever left Torrance after that.

Rosa fell in love with her gangly farmer, and I fell in love with his neighbor.

I fell in love, too, with corn fields and hot sun and the look of the stars when they blazed above them in a summer sky.

I lost a lot in meteor showers. A mother. A father. A best friend.

But for some reason, the tragedy could never touch the stars.

Because every time a star fell, I thought of my mother and I laying out on the ridge inside snow angels. And I heard her whisper in my ear. "They say that shooting stars are magic," she said. "Some people think that they have extra wishing powers. Other people think that they're alive."

I thought, too, of Rosa, and the choice she had made for me.

And so every time a star fell or even shone, I determined that I would wish with all the power in me for the ones I still had.

And when I married Ed Callahan, we named our daughter Stella.

I thought that we would have all the time in the world.

But one night, when Stella was very small, the stars fell over Torrance. I went running into the cornfields, chasing one of those falling stars.

Instead, I found Rosa.

She had changed in the years since we'd left Dackett.

She had grown maternal and warm and effusive. The shy, scared girl growing up under her mother's cruel shadow was gone. We'd spent long hours talking about her mother and about her people. All of the secrets of the Aster, she'd poured out to me.

And so I understood what she'd sacrificed when she hadn't sacrificed me.

So when I reached her there by the fallen rock, I felt no fear.

"Hi," I said.

She said nothing at first.

"I'm sorry, Maeve," she said.

I looked at her in confusion. And the light began to form around me. Just a haze at first. Golden and shimmering. It was beautiful.

"What changed?" I whispered.

"We all have to grow up someday," she said. On her chest, I caught the glint of a light. It was her mother's necklace-a diamond set into a shooting star.

And then the light grew brighter. And I knew.

"One for all," I whispered, desperately, imagining my Stella growing up without a mother, just as I had, claimed by the same monsters that had taken mine. I said the words, hoping that they would do what they'd done once upon a time so long ago. That they would save my life and save her soul.

"And all for one," Rosa said. But this time, the light only grew brighter.

About the Author

JOSH DYGERT'S short stories have appeared in a number of online magazines and anthologies, including in the #1 Amazon Bestselling Horror Anthology Secret Stairs. He is also the author of a middle-grade fantasy novel called The Story Traveler, which is available from Amazon. He studied English and Theater in college and now teaches middle school English. He can be found online at joshdygert.com.